PAMELA BROWN (1924–1989) was a British writer, actor, then television producer. She was just fourteen when she started writing her first book, and the town of Fenchester in the book is inspired by her home town of Colchester. During the Second World War, she went to live in Wales, so her first book, *The Swish of the Curtain*, was not published until 1941, when she was sixteen. She used the earnings from the books to train at RADA, and became an actor and a producer of children's television programmes.

Maddy
Again

PAMELA BROWN

PUSHKIN CHILDREN'S

Pushkin Press
71–75 Shelton Street
London WC2H 9JQ

Copyright © 2018 The Estate of Pamela Brown

Maddy Again was first published in Great Britain, 1956

First published by Pushkin Press in 2019

1 3 5 7 9 8 6 4 2

ISBN 13: 978-1-78269-193-8

Designed and typeset by Tetragon, London
Printed and bound by CPI Group (UK) Ltd, Croydon, CR0 4YY

www.pushkinpress.com

Maddy Again

NOTES ABOUT THE SETTING

Maddy Again was first published in the 1950s, and the following references may require some additional explanation for the modern reader.

Television was still in its infancy in the 1950s. Programmes were broadcast in black and white, and most were broadcast live.

Before decimalisation in 1971, British currency consisted of pounds, shillings, and pence:
    12 pennies = 1 shilling
    two and a half shillings = half a crown
    5 shillings = 1 crown
    20 shillings = 1 pound
    21 shillings = 1 guinea

A rep. (or repertory) company is a theatre company residing permanently at a particular theatre, regularly changing the performances on offer to their audiences.

Y.W.H.A. is the abbreviation for Young Women's Hostels Association.

The pictures means the cinema.

The *never-never* is a system of payment in which part of the cost of something is paid immediately, and then small regular payments are made until no more money is owed.

A.S.M. is an assistant stage manager.

I

ZILLAH

As Maddy rounded the corner and saw the Academy in the distance she was overtaken by her two best friends, Buster and Snooks. They fell on each other delightedly, and for a few minutes there was nothing but back-slapping and giggles.

'Did you have gorgeous Easter hols?' asked Buster, who was thin and weedy.

'Jolly exciting,' Maddy answered.

'We heard the broadcast from the Blue Door Theatre,' said Snooks. 'It was wonderful.'

For the rest of the way to the Academy Maddy told them what was happening in her home town of Fenchester, where her elder sister, Sandra, and her friends were running a repertory company. 'It was all so exciting that it seemed a pity to have to come back,' she finished up.

'I suppose when you're old enough to leave school you'll stay at Fenchester and work with the Blue Door Theatre Company,' said Snooks enviously.

'Yes, of course,' answered Maddy.

'So you'll never go up into the proper Academy?'

The British Actors' Guild Academy was divided into two parts. The junior department was for children of school age, and provided ordinary lessons as well as stagecraft, but the senior school was concerned entirely with stage subjects, such as voice production, diction, fencing and dancing. In order to get from the junior to the senior Academy it was necessary to pass a stiff entrance test, just as did the people coming from other schools.

'Don't expect I'd pass the test anyhow...' said Maddy.

Although for her age Maddy had had a considerable amount of stage and film experience, she did not always get on very well at the Academy, for she was inclined to speak her mind too freely and to do exactly what she thought she would do just when she wanted to do it. This did not make her particularly popular with her teachers.

'What did you two get up to in the holidays?' Maddy remembered to ask Snooks and Buster.

'We did some television; it was lovely. It all happened through the Academy. You see, some small, thin children were needed to be orphans in a play, and so Mrs Seymore suggested us, and we did it.'

'I've never done any television,' said Maddy enviously. 'Is it like filming?'

'Don't know,' said Snooks, 'I've never done any filming.'

By now they were outside the Academy, which stood in a quiet square lined with plane trees. It was a tall, grey house with stone lions at the door posts. The juniors were all devoted to this main building of the school, which had carved above the door, 'They have their exits and their entrances'. It was so much more exciting than the rather bleak schoolhouse round the corner where they did their lessons and which seemed to have a dusty, chalky atmosphere. Here in the main building there was always the noise of a piano being played, always the rise and fall of verse-speaking voices, and the thud of dancing classes in full swing.

'Wonder what this term will be like...' said Maddy as they went through the swing doors.

Inside was a seething mass of students from twelve-year-olds to twenty-year-olds, all talking at the top of their voices about what they had done in the holidays. Maddy and Buster and Snooks were soon submerged in a rush of their chattering friends, and the noise did not subside until they were sitting in the theatre, waiting for prayers, and Wainwright Whitfield, the principal of the Academy, strode on to the stage. Instantly there was silence, for the tall, grey-haired figure had a dignity that subdued even the faintest giggle.

Although Maddy had already spent several terms at the Academy, she was always impressed by the simple but effective service that was held every morning. No one was compelled to go. Attendance was entirely optional, and yet the theatre was always full.

The 'Babies', as the juniors were called, spent the mornings at the Academy, and after lunch went round to the schoolhouse for their lessons, from two o'clock until five. Then as often as not they were back again at the Academy to cram in an extra ballet lesson or rehearsal for a student production. Sometimes they had to do school lessons on

Saturday mornings in order to make up the requisite number of school hours.

Last term their class had been small—only a dozen of them—but this term the numbers had swollen to fifteen. Two of the newcomers were boys who had been at a choir school, but whose voices had just broken, and the third was a girl of striking appearance. She was about fifteen and had long dark hair, a peaches-and-cream complexion and beautiful dark blue eyes. She seemed absolutely paralysed by everything at the Academy. During prayers she sat with her head bowed so low that Maddy had thought she must be extremely devout, but now, while they sat waiting for their diction lesson to start, she sat in exactly the same posture, staring fixedly at the floorboards. Hers was such an unusual face that nobody could keep their eyes off the girl, and this made her more and more embarrassed. Apart from her face, her dress also attracted attention—it was so peculiar. Other students wore jeans, slacks, dungarees, kilts, practice tights—a most mixed collection—but the new girl was wearing a hideous tan-coloured velveteen dress with a lace collar. It was obviously home-made, and was many years out of fashion.

'Who on earth is she?' whispered some of the girls to each other, behind their hands.

The whispering ceased as Roma Seymore entered to give the class their diction lesson. She was grey-haired, with a pleasant face and the most beautiful voice imaginable. For the first few minutes she just chatted with the class, then she took the register. The names of the three new pupils had been added to the end of the list, so there was no doubt as to who was intended when Mrs Seymore came to the last name—Zillah Pendray.

Maddy pricked up her ears. The name rang a bell. She had heard it somewhere before—Zillah Pendray. The new girl raised her head and was staring in a hypnotised fashion at Mrs Seymore, but made no answer. Mrs Seymore looked round the room, then said sharply, 'Well, speak up, if you're here...'

All the others had answered 'Yes, Mrs Seymore,' 'Adsum,' 'Here' or whatever they chose, for it was a tradition to answer in the way they had been accustomed to at their previous schools. To everyone's amazement Zillah finally answered in a very small voice, 'I be here, thank you.'

There was an instant shout of laughter from the class. Mrs Seymore looked sharply at Zillah to see if she was trying to be funny, but seeing the hot flush that covered the girl's face and neck she made no comment. When the merriment had died down, to cause a diversion Mrs Seymore said, 'I'm pleased to be able to tell you that you are going to have a new class this term. The recent growth of television has convinced us that you should all learn something about the technique of television acting, as it is so different from that of the theatre. Therefore we have managed to get a T.V. producer to come along and give instruction. You younger ones may be directly concerned, because the demand for children on television is enormous. Now, two of you have done some already, haven't you? Let me see—Valerie and Gladys, wasn't it?' Valerie and Gladys were Buster and Snooks, under their real names. 'Which reminds me, Gladys, we must settle on a stage name for you, mustn't we? Your mother and father agree to you changing from Gladys Snooks, don't they?'

'Oh, yes,' said Snooks. 'They want me to, and everyone at the television studio said I simply must change it.'

'Have you or your parents any suggestions?' asked Mrs Seymore interestedly.

'Well,' said Snooks rather shyly. 'I had thought of Gloria de Silva—that keeps to my real initials, you see.'

Maddy giggled rudely. 'Snooks suits you better.'

Mrs Seymore tried not to smile. 'I think perhaps Gloria de Silva is going a little too far,' she said. 'Gloria would be quite suitable, I suppose, but what about a more everyday surname? Something beginning with S, if you like.'

The whole class began suggesting names, 'Smythe', 'Stanton', 'Sadler', 'Sutherland'.

'Sausage,' said Maddy hopefully.

'What about Stratford?' said Mrs Seymore. 'It has good theatrical connections.'

'People might think of Stratford East, instead of on-Avon,' said Gladys gloomily.

'But that Stratford—Stratford-atte-Bow—has a lovely old theatre,' said Mrs Seymore.

'I don't think I want to be called after a place,' objected Snooks. 'I'd rather be called after a person. What a pity your name is Seymore. Gloria Seymore sounds lovely.'

Mrs Seymore tried it over.

'Yes, it does. And I haven't acted for years. I tell you what, I'll lend it to you, Gladys. But you mustn't ever trade on it, will you?'

'Trade on it? Oh, you mean pretend I'm related to you. No, of course not, Mrs Seymore. Thank you ever so much for lending me the name.'

Snooks beamed all over her face.

The whole class buzzed with envy at anyone being given Mrs Seymore's name.

'Gloria Seymore.' Snooks tried it over. 'I feel better already, now that I'm not Gladys Snooks any more. Will you change it in the register, please, Mrs Seymore?'

'I still think Gloria Sausage is a name people would have remembered,' Maddy whispered to her.

'Now we've chatted long enough,' said Mrs Seymore. 'We must get on with some work. I'll hear your holiday tasks.'

Everybody groaned, not because they minded saying their pieces to Mrs Seymore, but because it had been such a difficult job to find time for learning during the holidays.

'Now, we will go round the class alphabetically. Beautiful diction, please.'

At the Academy they were so used to standing up and reciting Shakespeare and other poetry at all hours that any embarrassment at being called upon to do so had disappeared during their first term or so, and it had become a pleasure. The three newcomers, of course, were not in this happy position. One by one the others got up and recited Shelley's 'Ode to a Skylark' with great attention to clear vowels and sharp consonants. The newcomers thought that, as they had had no chance to prepare the piece, they would escape attention, but when all the old pupils had finished, Mrs Seymore turned to the two choir-school boys.

'Now I should like to hear you two do something—anything that you have learned by heart—it doesn't matter what. Who'll go first?'

The boys blushed and stuttered and looked at each other for inspiration.

'We don't—er—don't really know anything.'

'Well, what about one of the songs or hymns you used to sing at your old school; you must have learnt the words. Just say a few verses to me.'

Their performances were really rather funny. Speaking the lines was a totally different matter from singing them. They stumbled and forgot the words, and at times seemed about to burst into song. Their diction, however, was perfect, as they had been carefully trained at the choir school.

Then it was Zillah's turn. Everyone looked at her expectantly. The poor girl was going through agonies of fear and embarrassment.

'Now come along, dear, you know *something* by heart, I'm sure,' said Mrs Seymore encouragingly.

Zillah shook her head in silence.

'Some poetry, surely?'

'No. My dad doesn't hold with it,' she breathed.

Roma Seymore was shocked.

'Doesn't hold with poetry?'

'No.'

'Well, there must be something—nursery rhymes—does he hold with them?'

'No.'

'Well, the Bible then? Do you know anything from the Bible?'

Zillah nodded doubtfully.

'Well, I tell you what,' said Mrs Seymore kindly, 'you can have a few minutes to yourself to think about it. Go over there and sit by the window and just make sure you remember a few passages from the Bible, while the rest of us do some consonants exercises. There were some very lazy consonants in the "Ode to a Skylark". Now, everyone else, divide up into groups of three or four.'

In the confusion that always followed an order to divide up the class Maddy slipped across to Zillah. The fact that her father 'didn't hold with poetry' had jogged Maddy's memory.

'I say,' she whispered to Zillah. 'Do you know who I am?'

Zillah looked at her with wide, deep-blue eyes.

'Yes, you're Maddy.'

'How do you know?' Maddy demanded.

'They said you had short, fair pigtails, and you talked more than anyone else.'

'What a nerve!' snorted Maddy. 'You mean the Blue Doors, of course? They told me all about you, too—how Sandra, Vicky and Lyn met you in Cornwall and tried to persuade your father to let you come here for training. So he did let you come?'

'Yes,' said Zillah. 'And now I wish I hadn't.'

'Why?'

'I'm that frightened. London's so busy, and there's no grass. And I'm frightened of they escalators.'

'Don't worry,' said Maddy. 'You'll soon get used to it all. Where are you living?'

'At the Y.W.H.A. Dad arranged for me to go there.'

'But you were supposed to come to my digs—Mrs Bosham's. It's lovely there—she's a terrible cook, but ever so nice...'

'Maddy,' called Mrs Seymore. 'What are you doing? Talking as usual. Come back to your group. I really thought you might have improved a little this term.'

After they had gone through 'Peter Piper picked a peck of pickled pepper' a few times, Mrs Seymore said, 'Right, you can rest a while and we'll hear Zillah. Now, have you gone over a passage and made sure you know it?'

Zillah nodded.

'Good, well, stand up and face the class. Yes, now don't worry. It doesn't matter if you are not word perfect. I just want to hear your diction.'

Zillah's recitation from the Bible was a most extraordinary performance. Her voice was rich and warm and beautiful, and she said the Twenty-third Psalm with deep sincerity, but in the broadest West Country accent.

'Yes, of course,' said Mrs Seymore, when Zillah had finished. 'I remember you from the entrance tests. You won an award, didn't you?'

This was a polite way of saying that Zillah had gained a scholarship. Nevertheless, she blushed ashamedly.

'Jolly good,' murmured Maddy audibly, trying to show her that at the Academy it was considered an honour to be there on a scholarship.

'You are really rather a problem to me, Zillah,' said Mrs Seymore. 'Now, you do know that you have a very thick local accent, don't you?'

'Yes.' Zillah hung her head in shame.

'It is nothing to be ashamed of. It is a particularly musical accent, and your voice production is excellent. But I am supposed to teach you diction, and it is my job to get rid of that lovely accent of yours and make you speak like everyone else. For the first time in my life, I feel it will be a pity. But you must consider that there are so many parts that you could not play with an accent like that, and if you are going to be an actress, the greater variety of parts you can play, the better opportunity you have to make a living.'

Zillah did not seem able to take in this speech at all. She still looked miserable and uncertain.

'I think,' continued Roma Seymore, 'I will give you some private lessons to enable you to catch up with the rest of the class, and then I shan't have to devote a great deal of time to you in class. All right?'

Mrs Seymore smiled questioningly at Zillah, and Maddy willed Zillah to say thank you, but she didn't.

'Now we will go on with our consonant sounds,' said Mrs Seymore hurriedly, somewhat disconcerted by Zillah's lack of reaction.

When the lesson was over and they were going upstairs to fencing, Maddy caught up with Zillah and said, 'Do you like it at the Y.W.H.? Are the other girls friendly?'

Zillah looked a little surprised. 'I haven't spoken to any of them yet,' she said at last, 'but Miss Binns, the manageress, has told me I oughtn't to be there. She wants me to find somewhere else.'

'Oughtn't to be there! Why ever not?' demanded Maddy.

'Because I'm too young. They don't take girls under eighteen. They thought I was eighteen. I don't know who made the mistake, but Miss Binns doesn't want me to stay.'

'Then why don't you move into Mrs Bosham's? The Academy recommends her whenever young students have got to live on their own, because she adores coming out chaperoning if we do any work or anything. All the Blue Doors have lived at Mrs Bosham's.'

None of this made sense to Zillah, so Maddy said firmly, 'You come along with me this afternoon and we'll explain everything to Miss Smith, she's the Academy secretary. She's a dear, and I know she thinks the world of Mrs Bosham. She's bound to help. Probably she'll get on the phone to the Binns ogress and fix it all up for you to move to my place tomorrow. Snooks and Buster and I will come and help you with your bags.'

'I have but the one,' said Zillah slowly, then after a long pause added, 'It's right kind of you to take all this trouble. I only hope Dad won't be cross.'

When Maddy told Buster and Snooks what she had done they were not at all pleased.

'She's such a drear,' said Buster. 'She'll be a terrible handicap to us. I think you've made a great mistake, Maddy. Why ever did you do it?'

Maddy puckered her brow.

'We-ell—I knew that the rest of the Blue Doors had encouraged her—and I sort of—felt responsible. And she said she hadn't spoken to anyone at the Y.W.H.—can you imagine it!—and that they didn't want her there.'

'You are good, Maddy,' said Snooks earnestly.

Maddy shouted with laughter.

'That's about the first time in my life that anyone's called me good—it shows you're my true friend, Snooks—sorry, Miss Gloria Seymore.'

When Maddy went back to her digs in the evening she said, 'Oh, Mrs Bosham, I've let your empty room for you.'

Mrs Bosham was just serving the colourless soup, and she splashed down the ladle in the tureen saying, 'There now.'

Her round eyes, round nose and round mouth assumed an expression of disappointment. 'And I've just gorn and let it to a commercial gent. And you know I'd much rather 'ave students.'

'Oh, what a shame,' said Maddy. 'Well, could you let this girl share my room for a bit, till you've got a vacancy? There is room for another bed, and she's awfully lonely at the Y.W.H. Nobody's spoken to her yet, and she hasn't spoken to anyone, and she's frightened of escalators.'

'They don't have escalators in them Y.W.H.s, do they?' inquired Mrs Bosham, entirely missing the point.

'No, and no grass for her either.'

Mrs Bosham didn't understand this reference, but clicked her teeth sympathetically. 'The poor dear. Well, well!'

She picked up her eternal piece of knitting and started working furiously while Maddy drank her soup. Maddy had her evening meal earlier than the adult lodgers, because theoretically she went to bed before anyone else, but actually once she got down into Mrs Bosham's basement and started making toffee or telling Mrs Bosham the latest news from Fenchester, it was usually quite late before she could be chased upstairs to bed.

'Yes, well,' said Mrs Bosham after a few rows of purl and plain, 'I suppose we'd better let the poor duck share your room. I feel that sorry fer you lot, when you haven't got any parents in London, and you've got to be here to study. Is she younger than you are?'

'A bit older, I think,' said Maddy. 'But she seems awfully dopey in some ways. It's only because she's frightened,

I think. She's absolutely beautiful, but her clothes are awful. We'll have to smarten her up a bit.'

It seemed unlikely that Mrs Bosham could ever smarten anyone, for her own clothes, strained round her circular form, were completely timeless. She had worn them as long as anyone could remember, and seemed only to vary her headgear for different occasions—curlers for the morning, scarf or pixie hood for shopping and a rakish hat for really important occasions. 'Yes,' said Mrs Bosham, 'it'll be nice to have another youngster in the house. I still miss those brothers and sisters of yours y'know.' Mrs Bosham had never been able to sort out which of the Blue Doors were related to each other and which were not.

Next day, when Maddy told them that Zillah was to share her room, Buster and Snooks expressed their disgust in no uncertain terms.

'How can you! With someone who speaks like a farmer's boy,' said Snooks.

'Don't be such a snob,' Maddy rebuked her. 'And we can't all be Cockneys.'

Snooks snorted with rage. She came from Sutton, but Maddy always teased her about having a Cockney accent.

'You two are just jealous because you can't come and live at Mrs Bosham's,' Maddy went on.

'Jealous!' scoffed Buster. 'Some hopes! I'd rather die than live there. It smells of cabbage, and Mrs Bosham's hats are a disgrace. I'd much rather live at home.'

'Would you really?' said Maddy disbelievingly. 'I love Mrs Bosham's. Of course, home's nice too, but it's not London.'

Zillah just said, 'Oh', when they told her they would come and fetch her bags as soon as lessons were over.

'And my mother's sent me a food parcel, with one of her chocolate cakes, so we can have a feast this evening after supper,' added Maddy.

During the afternoon lessons, round in the schoolhouse, it became apparent that Zillah was a real dunce as far as school subjects were concerned. She could not do maths at all, had no idea of English grammar and knew no French. Maddy remembered that Sandra and Lyn and Vicky had told her that Zillah's parents had been constantly in trouble with the education authorities for keeping the girl away from school to help on the farm. In a small class like the 'Babies' her ignorance showed up appallingly, and she was quite definitely behind all the others, even those who were only twelve. By the end of the afternoon she was nearly in tears with shame.

'Don't worry,' Maddy whispered comfortingly in her ear. 'Lessons don't count—it's the acting classes that matter, and you know Mrs Seymore said you have a lovely voice.'

'I wish your sister and the others had never come to the village,' said Zillah bleakly. 'Until then I was quite happy at home with the animals and such.'

'You'll soon get over feeling homesick,' Maddy assured her. 'Come on, we'll go out and have a lovely tea at Raddler's, and then collect your bags.'

Raddler's was a little restaurant, over a baker's shop, near the Academy. The whole of the second floor was reserved for the Academy students, as the noise they made was so deafening that they could not be inflicted on the other patrons, who frequented the first floor. The older students allowed the

'Babies' to sit at one particular table, and when this became full they had to sit two on a chair, on each other's laps, or squat on the floor.

Zillah looked around the restaurant as though she were seeing the zoo at feeding time. Everyone tried to talk to her, and even some of the older students came over to have a look at her, but Maddy fended them off, and Buster and Snooks, too, found themselves coming to her defence.

After they had drunk glasses of milk and eaten innumerable sticky cakes, they walked down Tottenham Court Road window shopping. When they reached the Y.W.H. Maddy went up to the reception desk and said firmly, 'We've come for this little girl's luggage,' although Zillah towered above her by quite a head.

'Oh, yes,' said the clerk, 'I know all about it. Zillah can take you to her room.'

Zillah led the way up several flights of stairs until they reached her room. It was tiny, clean, light and airy, and looked totally un-lived in. In the middle of the floor was a small and very shabby old Gladstone bag.

'Is that all?' demanded Maddy.

'Yes,' said Zillah. 'I've only got my Sunday best.'

Snooks thought she had said 'Sunday vest' and giggled, but Maddy glared at her.

'Oh well, it's best to travel light. Come on.'

As there was nothing for Buster and Snooks to carry they decided to go home, and Maddy and Zillah set off for Mrs Bosham's. Maddy talked all the way, and was not particularly worried because Zillah did not answer, for she was quite used to people not saying much when she was talking.

Mrs Bosham took to Zillah immediately.

'What a good looker, eh?' she whispered audibly to Maddy behind Zillah's back and puffed upstairs with them to show how she had arranged the room.

'There now, I've given you a nice mattress on me divan from the droring-room. You can put your things in the top drawer of the chest, and there's room behind the curtain with Maddy's things fer you to hang yours. Oh well...' She glanced doubtfully at Zillah's bag. 'You won't need all that space, will you? Now, I've got a nice roly-poly for yer supper, and I'll give you a shout when it's ready.'

Zillah looked around the room, which had a view of roof-tops and chimney pots. Maddy had covered nearly every inch of the walls with pictures—of the Blue Doors, ballet pictures, photographs of her parents. The final result was cosy, if not artistic. Zillah gave what was almost a smile.

'Yes,' she said, 'it's nice here.'

Maddy felt greatly relieved.

'The supper will be awful,' she confided, 'but don't worry. I've got Mummy's cake up here, and we can have a private feast afterwards. It's lovely having someone to share with. Since the Blue Doors went I've had to have midnight feasts on my own, which isn't so much fun.'

Over supper, which was incredibly indigestible, Zillah began gradually to thaw out. She would make a remark in a very low voice, and then blush furiously, while Maddy and Mrs Bosham, who sat knitting in the corner, would pounce on it, elaborate it and talk for the next ten minutes before Zillah dared to make another observation.

On the pretext of going to bed early they went up and

polished off the chocolate cake, and when they had gone to bed Maddy said in the darkness, 'Do you think you're going to like it here?'

'Oh, yes,' replied Zillah gratefully. 'Everything is so comfortable.'

Maddy tried to imagine what Zillah's home must be like, if Mrs Bosham's boarding house struck her as comfortable, but went to sleep before she could get very far with the thought.

2

MR MANYWEATHER

As Friday and their first television lesson drew near, excitement among the 'Babies' mounted.

'Who is the teacher going to be?' Maddy asked Snooks.

'A Mr Manyweather,' said Snooks. 'Leon Manyweather. He's a famous television producer.'

'Did he produce the show you were in?'

'No, a lady produced ours.'

'We must wear our best clothes tomorrow,' announced Maddy, and it was a very smart 'Babies' class that turned up at the Academy on Friday. Zillah had been the only problem.

'Shall I wear my Sunday?' she had asked Maddy.

As her 'Sunday', a particularly unpleasant mauve velvet, was slightly more hideous than her tan-coloured everyday dress, Maddy said hastily, 'Oh, no, I don't think I should be as formal as that.'

For once, Maddy laid aside her favourite red slacks, put on a new pale-blue summer dress and white socks, and even cleaned her shoes. By the time she had finished with it, her hair, too, looked less like a bird's nest than usual.

Their lesson with Mr Manyweather was to be the last before lunch, and when they trooped into the classroom they found nobody there except a young man with a thatch of reddish hair and large spectacles, who was thumping out some jazz on the rickety piano.

His playing was more enthusiastic than accurate, but he seemed to be enjoying himself. He finished with a clash of discords and swung round on the piano stool to face the class.

'Hullo. Are you the Babies? You're bigger than I expected from the name. My name's Manyweather.'

Their jaws dropped in astonishment, and there were a few stifled giggles.

'Now, I'm supposed to teach you about television. It's a big subject, and nobody knows all about it yet. I wonder how much you know already? How many of you have television sets at home?'

Half a dozen hands were raised.

'And how many of you have acted on television?'

Buster and Snooks raised their hands importantly.

'Good. Well, I hope more of you will have a chance before long. Now, first of all I'm going to try and give you a rough idea of how television works. And for that I'll have to draw on the blackboard. But don't be alarmed. It's not a bit dull.'

It wasn't. His drawing was very eccentric, but he livened up his diagrams with little matchstick men with 'balloons' coming out of their mouths saying, 'I am a cameraman' or 'I am a producer.' A lot of pupils did not understand the technical details of what Mr Manyweather was saying, but

26

they listened eagerly because of the flow of jokes and the funny drawings.

When the lesson was nearly over he said, putting down the chalk with a large gesture, 'Well, I don't suppose you're any the wiser, but that's *my* idea of how television works. We haven't even got round to the technique of television acting, but before we finish for the day I'd like to see each of you do something, so that I can feel I know you a bit. Now, all I want from you at the moment is sincerity. The camera does not lie. A television camera can see right into your soul through the windows of your eyes. You don't need any tricks—any theatrical gestures—hardly any voice even. All you need—or nearly all—is sincerity. Try to remember those points when you do your party piece for me.'

He pointed to people at random, but there was only time for a few before the end of the lesson. After each performance he said much the same thing.

'No, much too big. Too many gestures. Too theatrical. I know that you have been used to the theatre up till now, but you've got to forget everything you've learned and start again for television.'

The only performance he liked was from the younger of the choir-school boys, who did a speech from *Henry V.* Up till now he had been accused of underacting, but this seemed to suit Mr Manyweather. 'Jolly dee,' he said. 'Just the job. Now do you see what I mean?' he appealed to the others. 'Very quiet, very untheatrical, quite sincere.'

Then Maddy was called upon. 'Come on, Gretchen. You next.'

'My name's Maddy...'

'I never call people by their names; I call them what they look like. You've got fair plaits like a little Dutch girl, so I shall call you Gretchen.'

Maddy did a speech of Maria's from *Twelfth Night* and when she had finished Mr Manyweather laughed kindly and said, 'Well, I can see you're a comedienne, but that was much too broad—much, much too broad. But don't worry. We'll soon get you toned down enough for a television camera. Now, then, what about Velia?'

Everyone glanced round the room to see who Velia might be. It made life interesting, no one being called by their correct names.

'The witch of the wood,' giggled Maddy. 'Who's that, Mr Manyweather?'

Then she saw that he was indicating Zillah.

'What's your name?' he asked her.

'Zillah. Zillah Pendray.'

'What a wonderful name. I was almost right, wasn't I?'

Zillah did a speech of Cordelia's which Maddy had made her learn, telling her that she could not go on saying the Twenty-third Psalm for ever, and when it was finished Mr Manyweather looked at her speculatively for a long time.

'Interesting,' he said at last. 'Very interesting. Excellent for television in a way—no tricks, no gestures, very sincere, but your accent, of course, makes you quite impossible in a speech like that. Learn some Joan of Arc for next week, will you, please? Then I shan't be distracted by the accent. And everyone, for next week please prepare something specially for me. I *don't* want any old speech that you've known for

28

years, just polished up. I want you to prepare something entirely new, remembering what I've told you today. O.K.?'

They all agreed enthusiastically. The bell rang, and Mr Manyweather put on a very shabby duffle coat, picked up an even shabbier briefcase, together with a frying pan inadequately wrapped in paper, a roll of music and a shooting stick, and disappeared, crying, 'See you next week.'

'What a funny man,' said Maddy when he had gone.

'Isn't he *young*?' chorused everyone, and immediately started discussing what speeches they would learn for the following Friday.

'I wish next Friday was tomorrow,' said Maddy impatiently. 'I want to learn more about television. It sounds such fun.'

While they were eating ham rolls in the canteen, where you had to shout in order to be heard above the din, Maddy said to Snooks, 'You've got television at home, haven't you?'

'Yes,' said Snooks casually. 'Why?'

'We haven't. Neither at home in Fenchester, nor at Mrs Bosham's. I've hardly ever seen any. Have you, Zillah?'

'No. Never.'

Maddy turned to Snooks again.

'There you are, Zillah's never seen it, and I have hardly ever.'

'Well, I can't help it...' began Snooks, then saw the light. 'Oh, I see. Yes. Do come to tea tomorrow and watch television. Saturday's is usually a good programme.'

'Oh, thanks,' said Maddy with satisfaction. 'Had you better ask your mother? Ring her up, I mean?'

'No,' said Snooks. 'I often have people in on a Saturday afternoon—usually friends from my old school. I've never had any from the Academy before.'

She looked doubtfully at Maddy and Zillah.

'It's all right,' said Maddy. 'I'll wear this dress and lend Zillah a blouse and skirt, if she'd like. You *would* like to come to tea, wouldn't you?' she demanded, noting Zillah's expression of terror.

Zillah nodded miserably, and Snooks turned her eyes up to the ceiling in despair.

Maddy was extremely pleased at having secured an invitation, for in London weekends were rather a problem. She could not often afford the fare to Fenchester, and it was very dull at Mrs Bosham's when there was no Academy to go to. And going out, though nice, was expensive.

Snooks gave them minute details of how to get to her house, and when she noticed Buster looking wistful she included her in the invitation as well.

'Which shall we call you at home, Gladys or Gloria?' demanded Maddy.

'Gladys, I'm afraid.'

'O.K. We'll try to remember.'

'My mother's not particular about it, though,' said Snooks. 'She's not particular about anything really—except about not wearing high heels with slacks.'

Maddy thought she must be rather a remarkable mother, and couldn't wait to see her.

When Mrs Bosham heard that the two girls were going out to tea she was delighted.

'It'll be nice fer you,' she said, 'to see a bit of life.'

'We're going to watch television,' Maddy told her.

'Coo, have they got the telly? I wonder whether I ought to get one—on the never-never, you know. The lodgers often ask, when they first come, 'ave I got the telly. If I'ad, I could put me terms up...'

She pondered on it, and Maddy said, 'Well, it would be a good idea to *have* it, but not to put your terms up, because then no one from the Academy could afford to come here...'

'Oh, I wouldn't put them up fer the students—only fer the commercials.'

'That's right,' urged Maddy. 'Then the students could look at the television that the commercials were paying for!'

Next day Maddy had a hard job to persuade Zillah to accept the loan of any clothes.

'I'll wear my Sunday,' she insisted. 'That's what it's for— going visiting...'

'But it's too dressy,' said Maddy desperately.

'Don't you like it?' Zillah looked hurt. 'It's new. My mother made it—specially for London.'

'I should keep it,' said Maddy, inspired, 'for wearing on the stage. If we do a modern play at the end of the term, we have to provide our own clothes, you know.'

'Do we? Then I'd better. But can I wear my everyday...'

'Here, borrow a white blouse of mine, and my grey skirt.'

'It'll be too short...'

It was, but the white blouse suited her so well that Maddy persuaded her to wear the outfit.

'You can wear my grey blazer too, and it looks almost like a suit, you see. I'll take my mackintosh in case it rains.'

'Mother's making me a real summery frock for later on,' said Zillah. 'So I shan't need to borrow anything again.'

They set out early to make sure of getting to Snooks's in time. In fact, they started before lunch, and Mrs Bosham gave them some sandwiches to eat in the train. Zillah was terrified of Victoria Station, with all the bustle and scurrying people, and the constant train noises. She was quite pale, and Maddy had to take her by the arm and drag her along. They caught the train with plenty of time to spare, and found an empty carriage. As soon as they sat down Maddy suggested they should eat their sandwiches—'before they got stale'. Mrs Bosham was not a very good sandwich cutter—the bread was too thick and the meat was too lumpy, and apt to fall out. They both agreed that she was not so good at sandwiches as their own mothers.

'Where are we now?' Zillah kept demanding, once the train had started.

'London still,' Maddy kept replying.

'Isn't it big,' cried Zillah. 'Where does it end?'

Maddy was amazed to find that not only had Zillah never been to London before she came to the Academy, but until then had never left her village of Polgarth.

'*Never?*' inquired Maddy incredulously.

'No. Never. Dad used to go over to town to market, but he never took Mum and me...'

'Goodness!' Maddy snorted. 'Didn't you insist?'

'You don't know my Dad!' said Zillah darkly.

When they reached Sutton, Snooks was at the station to meet them, waving and shouting 'Yoo-hoo' with as much excitement as though she hadn't seen them for six months.

'We didn't think you'd expect us quite so early,' said Maddy.

'I guessed you'd come in good time,' said Snooks. 'It's a long way to our house. Shall we take a bus or walk?'

'Walk,' said Maddy. 'There's plenty of time, isn't there? I mean, television doesn't start yet, does it?'

'No. Not for ages.'

They dawdled along, looking in shop windows and talking and giggling, until Snooks said, 'Oh, help, I'd forgotten Buster. She'll probably be waiting at home. We'd better get a move on.'

They hurried along to Snooks's house, where Buster, looking very clean and tidy, was sitting rather stiffly on a settee talking to Mrs Snooks. Mrs Snooks was large and pretty and nicely dressed, and determined to put her daughter's friends at their ease.

'I'm having my tea in here,' she said. 'I've laid yours in the dining-room. I'm sure you'll like to have it by yourselves, won't you? And afterwards you can come in here to watch the television.'

'Will you call us immediately it starts, even if we haven't finished?' asked Snooks anxiously.

'Yes,' laughed Mrs Snooks. 'Do you really mean that the programme's more important than food?'

'Oh, yes,' said Snooks and Buster promptly. And even Maddy agreed.

The tea was enormous and delicious, including jelly and blancmange and three sorts of cake, but the girls hurried through it, so that they were back in the lounge when the children's television started.

They sat in a row on low humpties and stools and watched in earnest silence from beginning to end, except when Snooks put in, 'This bit isn't as good as usual,' or 'This is a new item—I've never seen her before.'

33

The first part of the programme was a band show, with some children singing and dancing, and the second was a play, in which there were two boys and three girls, all about twelve years old.

When it was over and Mrs Snooks had switched off, Maddy said, 'H'mm, wasn't bad, was it? But we could be as good as that, don't you think? Where do they get the kids from?'

'Other schools like ours,' said Buster. 'I know, because we met some when we did our show.'

'Did you like it, Zillah?' asked Maddy, trying to bring her into the conversation, for she had hardly spoken since she arrived. 'Did you like it better than the pictures?'

Zillah looked at Maddy blankly.

'I've never been to the pictures.'

'*Never* been to the *pictures*?' they all repeated.

'My dear child,' cried Mrs Snooks, 'where have you lived?'

Zillah was so embarrassed that Maddy told her life story for her—as much as she had heard from the Blue Doors—occasionally saying to Zillah, 'That's right, isn't it?' 'No, no,' Zillah would reply frantically when Maddy's imagination roamed too far from the truth.

Mrs Snooks was fascinated, and looked at Zillah as though she were some strange animal.

'You poor little thing,' she said. 'Now you're here we must see that you do go out. Shall we all go to the cinema tonight—just to show Zillah?'

'Oh, yes,' they all cried, and made a dash for the evening paper to see what was being shown locally. Finally they decided on an exciting double-feature programme, which included a cowboy film and a comedy. Before they got ready for the cinema Snooks took them all round her home, and Zillah saw for the first time a refrigerator, an electric hairdryer and a washing machine.

'Isn't it a lovely house!' she breathed to Maddy, who agreed, but secretly thought she would probably prefer the farmhouse at Polgarth, which was Zillah's home. Snooks's house was very comfortable but awfully *ordinary*, she felt.

When they went into the cinema the cowboy film had started, and as they stepped into the darkness of the auditorium there was the sound of hooves, and stampeding wild horses seemed to leap out of the screen at them. Zillah gave a scream of terror, and made to run back into the foyer. Maddy grabbed her by the arm.

'Don't be silly. It's only on the screen.'

'But it's so... so big.'

It surprised Maddy to hear someone complaining that the cinema screen was too big. She had heard that people used to the cinema often found a television screen too small, until they became accustomed to it, but she had never heard of anyone who objected to the size of a cinema screen.

At the end of the programme they were all bleary-eyed and exhausted and it was very late. Poor Zillah had dark rings under her eyes and looked as if she were half asleep.

'It was wonderful,' she said to Mrs Snooks. 'I can never thank you properly.'

Mrs Snooks laughed a little and straightened her smart hat.

'My dear child,' she said, 'I'm so glad you've enjoyed it. I'm afraid it's so late that there isn't time for you to come back for supper, so we'd better all see you and Maddy on to the train, then we'll walk home with Buster.'

35

In the train Zillah fell asleep and slept all the way to Victoria. Maddy studied her carefully. She really was a strange girl! Asleep, she looked so beautiful that it was difficult to realise she was so... so simple when she was awake. And how did she manage to be such a good actress, when she had never been to a cinema—let alone a theatre? In some ways she was rather a liability to have around, because she seemed so dumb, and yet there was a great satisfaction in showing her things for the first time.

It was so late when they reached Fitzherbert Street that Mrs Bosham was quite worried.

'Thought you'd bin kidnapped,' she cried when she opened the door.

'My father always says that if anybody ever kidnaps me they'll soon send me back,' laughed Maddy as they went inside.

'Did you 'ave a good time?'

'We've watched television *and* been to the pictures,' said Maddy.

'And seen a refrigerator!' added Zillah, with shining eyes.

Mrs Bosham had the grace not to laugh.

'Well I never! What a day. Now off to bed, both of you, and I'll bring you up a nice supper. What would you like to eat?'

'We had an enormous tea,' said Maddy. 'But perhaps a little something...'

They ate slices of Mrs Bosham's home-made cake, which was of a soggy consistency, and Maddy said, 'What shall we do to-morrow?'

''Tis the Sabbath,' said Zillah picturesquely.

'Er—yes,' said Maddy. 'So 'tis.'

But it sounded different when she said it.

'I go to Chapel,' said Zillah. 'Is there a chapel in London?'

'There must be,' said Maddy. 'Would St Paul's count, I wonder?'

'St Pauls's—that be a cathedral...'

'*Is* a cathedral,' Maddy corrected her. 'Not *be* a cathedral. You don't mind if I correct you?'

'No, surely, I don't. That *is* a cathedral. I'd dearly love to see it. Would it be so very wicked to go, think you?'

Zillah was constantly amazing Maddy.

'*Wicked!* To go to a cathedral! Oh, Zillah, of course not,' Maddy assured her.

'Are you sure? Everything's so different in London,' said Zillah in a bewildered fashion. 'Isn't it all worshipping idols, though?'

'We'll go to St Paul's tomorrow,' said Maddy firmly. 'And then you'll see...'

Next day was beautifully sunny, and Mrs Bosham decided to accompany them, leaving the joint and potatoes to roast in the oven. Zillah wore her 'Sunday', Mrs Bosham wore her best and most atrocious hat, and for once Maddy looked quite subdued beside them.

'How do we get there?' demanded Zillah.

'I dunno, I never bin.'

'Never been? And you've lived in London all your life! Really, you two are a fine pair,' Maddy told them. 'You'd never get anywhere without me.'

Nevertheless, under Maddy's guidance, they took two wrong buses and the service had started by the time they arrived. They were all extremely impressed by it, especially Zillah.

'It's ever so different from Chapel,' she whispered.

When the service was over they stood on the steps and watched the congregation depart. There were visitors of every race and colour.

'Look at all the black people,' cried Zillah delightedly.

'Sh!' Maddy hissed at her, as though she were a small child. 'They'll hear you and be hurt. Do you really mean to say you've never seen any coloured people before...?'

'No, we never had them in Polgarth.'

Zillah was the only person who made Maddy feel old.

When they got back to Fitzherbert Street, on the right bus this time, the Sunday dinner was cooked to a turn, and Maddy and Zillah ate theirs with the other lodgers, in the dining-room. This was the only meal of the week at which they met the others, and Maddy always enjoyed it enormously, chattering sixteen to the dozen to the 'commercials' and the university students who made up the rest of Mrs Bosham's household. Zillah huddled in her chair, however, keeping her eyes on her plate, and looking terrified that someone might speak to her.

The girls were so replete after lunch that they went and lay in Regent's Park, and worked on their speeches for Mr Manyweather.

'It's no good my doing a serious speech,' said Maddy. 'He says I'm a comedienne, so I shall have to be one.'

And she chose a comedy speech from *Junior Miss*, which she proceeded to rehearse with an American accent.

Zillah did her Saint Joan speech several times, and Maddy was very much impressed by it. But to her amazement Zillah asked after a while, 'Who *was* Joan of Arc?'

'Who was Joan of Arc?' ejaculated Maddy. 'Goodness, girl, didn't you *ever* go to school? She was—she was—well, she was Saint Joan,' she finished lamely.

'But where did she live?'

'Oh, for heaven's sake read the whole play and find out. I can't understand how anyone can deliver that speech as well as you do, and yet not know who Saint Joan was.'

Maddy was quite indignant about it.

'If Mr Manyweather found out you didn't know he'd be furious.'

So Zillah spent the rest of the afternoon reading Bernard Shaw, while Maddy yapped away beside her in an infuriating juvenile American accent.

The 'Babies' worked on their speeches all the week, to the detriment of their other homework, and when Friday came everyone was determined to impress Mr Manyweather. He turned up late for the lesson, as untidy as he had been the previous week, saying, 'Now, we must get a move on or we shan't get through. And I particularly want to hear you all because this week there's a prize—one for a boy and one for a girl.'

His pupils looked towards the strange assortment of parcels he was carrying. Whatever could the prizes be?

'That knobbly-shaped one looks nice,' whispered Maddy to Snooks. 'I'd like to win that one.'

'I think it's books,' said Snooks. 'He's got lots of books with him.'

All did their best to remember what Mr Manyweather had told them the previous week. They didn't use large gestures, they didn't use too much voice, they tried not to overact, but at one moment Colin, the elder of the choir-school boys, suddenly made a sweeping gesture of pointing right into the distance, and then looked at his own finger in a horrified fashion. Everybody roared with laughter, including Mr Manyweather.

'I'm sorry,' Colin said. 'That one got away by mistake. I learnt it in Shakespeare.'

Zillah was already shaking with apprehension, and Maddy, too, was unusually nervy as her turn approached.

'Come on, Little-by-little,' said Mr Manyweather, and Eric, the younger choir-school boy, resigned to this nickname all his life, stood up and did his speech. Mr Manyweather had approved of him last week, and this time he was obviously even more delighted.

'He's won the boy's prize all right,' whispered Maddy. 'Go on Zillah, you get the girl's.'

But poor Zillah was so nervous she dried in the middle. She just could not remember, and had to give up, although she had said her speech perfectly a dozen times to Maddy.

'What a shame. It would have been good,' said Mr Manyweather regretfully, 'very good. Still, I'd rather have people nervous than feeling nothing. You'll learn to control it.'

Although they had both appeared on television, neither Buster nor Snooks put up a very good show. They both overacted, and Mr Manyweather told them they appeared affected, which made them very crestfallen.

Maddy's stomach was turning over in a most unpleasant fashion, when Mr Manyweather said, 'Come on, Gretchen, it's your turn.'

She gave a covetous look at the knobbly parcel on the floor beside his briefcase, and got up and did her *Junior Miss* speech, trying not to overdo the comedy. Her American accent was hideous, and very funny, and all the class began to giggle. She kept her voice at a conversational level, and directed her speech at one imaginary person standing quite close to her.

The whole class clapped when she had finished, and Mr Manyweather roared with laughter.

'What a little horror!' he cried. 'I've never seen anything so nauseating, but excellent!'

The last few speeches were not particularly good, and Maddy began to feel excited.

'You've got it—you've got it,' whispered Buster and Snooks.

'Whatever can it be?' thought Maddy.

'Well, that's that,' said Mr Manyweather. 'You've all worked jolly hard, I can see that. Now who shall have the prizes?'

'Eric and Maddy,' cried several voices.

'Yes, that's what I think,' said Mr Manyweather. 'I'm glad you all agree. Now, Maddy—and Eric.'

They stood up, and the class clapped and Maddy looked to see which parcels he would pick up. But he didn't pick up any.

'Your prize,' he told them, 'will be a visit to the television studios.'

3

'AGATHA'

Amidst the buzz of envy and congratulations Maddy asked, 'Which sort of television, B.B.C. or commercial?'

'B.B.C. probably,' said Mr Manyweather. 'I work for both sides; I'm a free-lance. I'll let you know next week when and where it will be. I shall have to ask well in advance, because they don't really like visitors. The studios are cluttered up enough already.'

Just then the bell rang for the end of the period, and picking up his parcels Mr Manyweather departed in his usual flurry, before Maddy could inquire what was in the knobbly one.

Everybody crowded round Eric and Maddy and told them how lucky they were.

'You will behave nicely, won't you?' urged Rosalind, who was the eldest in the class, and therefore thought it her duty to say big-sisterly things on every occasion. 'The honour of the Academy will be at stake.'

'Of course I shall,' said Maddy. 'What do you expect me to do? Turn cartwheels in front of the cameras?'

'Oh, you mustn't,' cried Buster. 'They'd be furious!'

'Don't worry,' said Eric. 'I'll see she doesn't let the side down.'

'And wear something decent,' urged Rosalind, eyeing Maddy's scarlet slacks with disfavour.

The next week went very slowly indeed, and Maddy kept on saying to Zillah, 'I wonder when it will be. Do you think it will be soon?' until Zillah nearly screamed.

When the time came for the next lesson Maddy was hopping up and down in the doorway, waiting to greet Mr Manyweather.

'When is it?' she cried, as soon as he appeared.

'When is what?' he asked vaguely, blinking behind his thick spectacles.

'When are you taking us to the studio? Oh, you haven't changed your mind,' wailed Maddy.

'Oh, that. Yes, of course, I haven't told you. It's tomorrow.'

'Tomorrow!' cried Maddy. 'I'll never be ready in time.'

Mr Manyweather laughed. 'Why, what have you got to do?'

'Well, clean my shoes for one thing...'

'I shouldn't bother,' said Mr Manyweather. 'After all, you won't be going in front of the cameras.'

Maddy looked at *his* shoes. They were badly in need of polish.

Before they started the lesson he played the piano for a little while, and they all danced like dervishes.

'That's fine,' he said when they were all exhausted. 'Now we'll be able to concentrate better. Today I've brought a plan of a television studio so that you can all look at it, and Gretchen and Little-by-little won't feel quite so lost tomorrow. Here, I'll pin it on the blackboard, and you can all come and study it.'

The plan was divided up into quarter-inch squares, with a number of strange shapes and patterns drawn on it that conveyed absolutely nothing to the students. Mr Manyweather pointed out which lines represented settings, and which shapes were cameras and microphones.

'Now you'll see that it's not a bit like the theatre, where one scene is set after the other on the same stage. For television there are acting areas all round the studio, and the poor actor has to do a steeplechase from one to the other, very often changing his clothes en route, and trying not to look puffed when he gets there. Then he's also got to take the cue from the floor manager to start the next scene, without showing that he's taking it. By that I mean the floor manager waves at him to start, but he mustn't wave back, because by that time the camera's on him.'

Buster and Snooks laughed delightedly, because they knew what he was talking about.

'Why do they have the floor manager to give the cue, instead of using a green light as they do in sound broadcasting?' asked Eric, who had done some radio work with his choir.

'Because a human being can get into some very odd corners and contrive to give cues where you couldn't possibly rig up a green cue light. And also the floor manager is in direct communication with the producer, who sits up in the control room, and talks from there to the floor manager, who hears him through headphones. The producer watches all that is happening on a lot of little television sets, called monitors, that are ranged in front of him. There is one monitor for every camera and the producer tells the vision mixer which camera's picture to transmit. He also speaks to the cameramen, who can hear him on *their* headphones, telling them what sort of shots he wants. Do you follow?'

He saw from their blank faces that they did not.

'Oh well, there's nothing else for it. You'll all have to come round the studios, a few at a time. But only as a reward for good work.'

Everyone cheered loudly. Mr Manyweather spent the remainder of the lesson trying to explain the studio plan, and pointing out the drawbacks and the advantages of acting for television, as compared to the theatre. At the end of the class he turned to Eric and Maddy.

'Meet me at a quarter to two outside Marble Arch Tube Station tomorrow afternoon. It doesn't matter what you wear—no one will be looking at you, but I should wear *soft* shoes in preference to clean ones, Maddy.'

'But I must wear a decent dress,' said Maddy, when he had gone. 'Why, I might be *discovered*.'

That evening there was great activity at 37 Fitzherbert Street. Maddy washed her hair, and dried it in front of the fire in Mrs Bosham's basement. Then she had a good scrub in the battered old bath where flakes of enamel came off and stuck to her. And then she sat up in bed cleaning shoes and doing her voice production exercises.

'Moo—mah—may,' she intoned.

'You sound like a sick cow,' Zillah laughed.

'You are insulting,' said Maddy hotly, until she remembered that Zillah was probably more familiar with sick cows than voice production exercises. 'Will you be all right by yourself tomorrow?' asked Maddy anxiously, for it would be the first time Zillah had been alone since she left the hostel. 'What will you do?'

'Go for a walk, I expect,' said Zillah vaguely.

'I don't know what time I shall be back,' said Maddy. 'Mr Manyweather didn't say.'

She took all the morning to get ready, because buttons kept coming off and she couldn't sew the clean collar on to her dress without getting it crooked. 'Oh, Mummy— why aren't you here?' she said aloud in desperation, and Zillah said, 'Here—I'll do it. You hold your needle like a pitchfork.'

Maddy was very pleased to hear Zillah speak like this. It meant that she was beginning to make the same sort of derogatory remarks that other people made to her, and that was a very good sign.

They had lunch early, and Zillah offered to walk down to the Tube with Maddy.

'You can tell 'em I'm thinking of buying one,' laughed Mrs Bosham from the doorstep.

'What on earth—oh, I see, a "telly",' said Maddy, as they set off down Fitzherbert Street.

'Don't get run over,' Maddy warned Zillah as she left her at the entrance to Tottenham Court Road Tube Station, for Zillah had an unnerving habit of plunging straight into the traffic without looking to left or right, and just hoping it would stop for her.

In the Tube train Maddy felt so excited and happy that she kept bursting out into grins, and then feeling foolish because people looked at her.

Eric was waiting for her outside the Tube station at Marble Arch, looking extremely clean and neat, with his hair plastered down very close to his head.

'You look like a seal today,' Maddy told him. 'All shiny.'

'And you don't look a bit like yourself,' he told her.

'Thanks,' said Maddy, accepting this as the compliment it was meant to be.

They stood looking down the Tube steps, expecting Mr Manyweather to come up, but he did not appear.

'Supposing he's forgotten!' Maddy suggested in an agonised voice. 'I think he's a little eccentric, don't you? He might easily have forgotten.'

Suddenly a series of explosions made them look round into Oxford Street, and there stood the most extraordinary-looking vehicle they had ever seen. It was large, with a Rolls-Royce bonnet, but the open body was built of wood and had a home-made look—and inside were long wooden benches facing each other, giving a boat-like effect. The whole thing was built very high, and perched up at the wheel was Mr Manyweather waving violently to them, while clouds of blue smoke issued from the exhaust.

'No!' cried Eric. 'It can't be...'

'It is!' shouted Maddy. 'I didn't know he'd got a car...'

'And *what* a car!' said Eric, hurrying to inspect it from all angles before he got in.

'Hullo,' cried Mr Manyweather. 'Sorry I'm late—lost a wheel in the middle of Oxford Street.'

He roared with laughter, as though this were the most delicious joke.

'Jump in.'

Maddy had to climb over the front seat on to the rear portion, where she clung to the side for dear life, as Mr Manyweather started off in a determined manner to plunge into the traffic going round the circus at Marble Arch.

'What a magnificent job this is,' said Eric, bouncing about on the seat beside Mr Manyweather.

'I made her myself,' beamed Mr Manyweather. 'Hardly cost anything. Mind you, she eats up the petrol. But then, she holds a lot of people.'

'Masses of people, I imagine. How many is the most you have ever got into it?'

'Oh, about twenty, I should think. Mind you, it's not good for her springs...'

Maddy only just prevented herself from saying, '*Are* there any springs?' for she was bouncing about like a jack-in-the-box.

'I call her Agatha—I think it suits her personality.'

The journey to the B.B.C. studios at Shepherd's Bush was hair-raising. Mr Manyweather was a remarkably casual driver, and would take his hands off the wheel to gesticulate, or in order to point out some object of interest they were passing.

At Shepherd's Bush Green they got tangled up so badly in the traffic that they had to round the Green twice before they could get out of it.

'Mustn't grumble,' said Mr Manyweather, 'it gives us a chance to drink in the beauty of the scene. Now, the next problem is—somewhere to park.'

They drove up and down a grey little street where there was no sign of a studio, but where cars and motorbikes and motor scooters were parked nose to tail as far as one could see in either direction.

'Oh well, this'll do,' said Mr Manyweather, backing rather suddenly into a gateway bearing a large white sign, 'No Parking'.

'Can you really leave it here?' asked Eric anxiously.

'Yes,' said Mr Manyweather, climbing over the side of the car, as his door had stuck. He blinked short-sightedly at the notice.

'I can't read what that notice says; can you?' And without waiting for a reply he hustled them away down the street.

It seemed a very long walk to the studios.

'But where are they?' Maddy kept demanding.

At last they rounded a corner and a large white building seemed to spring up out of nowhere. 'How funny,' said Maddy. 'It didn't appear to be there a moment ago.'

The commissionaire at the door smartly saluted Mr Manyweather, who said, 'Hullo, Jo. How does it go?' and then led the way through the doors into the foyer.

'Good afternoon, Mr Manyweather,' fluted the receptionist, who looked as elegant as a fashion model. 'Do you require dressing-rooms?' she asked Maddy and Eric.

'No,' answered Mr Manyweather. 'They're just visiting. Can we have our passes, please. They're in my name.'

The receptionist flipped through a lot of cards and then handed him two.

'Many thanks,' said Mr Manyweather. 'Now, Gretchen, where shall we go first?'

'Where they actually do it,' said Maddy.

'O.K., where they do it.'

He led the way to a very small lift into which a number of people were trying to cram themselves, and said to the lift man, 'Hullo, Bert, we want to go to where they actually do it. Which studio is the busiest at the moment?'

'They're all madhouses today,' said Bert miserably, as a large lady wearing a shepherdess's dress struggled into the lift.

Mr Manyweather led the way through a heavy padded door marked 'No Smoking. No Admittance. No Visitors' into an enormous, high-roofed studio that was in such a state of confusion that at first Eric and Maddy just stood and blinked. Under very strong bright lights myriads of people were milling about among a jumble of huge cameras and microphones hung on the ends of 'fishing rods', attached to enormous trolleys, each worked by several men. But the strangest thing was the almost complete silence. The only sound in the whole vast studio was of a soprano singing in a small voice, with a piano accompanying her, right over at the far end of the studio. Because it was so quiet Maddy immediately wanted to giggle. She was glad that she was wearing rubber-soled shoes, as Mr Manyweather had suggested.

'Hold it!' somebody shouted suddenly, and the singing stopped, and pandemonium broke out. People shouted, people hammered, people rushed about. A make-up girl in a blue overall hurried over to powder the soprano's face, and Maddy turned to Mr Manyweather with shining eyes.

'Isn't it all exciting? Do tell us what is happening.'

'Well, this is just a rehearsal,' he explained. 'It's not being transmitted until this evening. That's why there's all this stopping and starting. It's to get the positions of the cameras and the booms correct. The booms are the things with the mikes on the end. You see, as I showed you on the plan, that the settings are arranged round the studio—and the cameras and the artistes move round to each in turn.'

Maddy and Eric had a good look.

'And the man standing in the middle of the floor wearing headphones is the floor manager. I told you about him, remember.'

'He's listening through his headphones to what the producer says, isn't he?' demanded Maddy.

'That's right.'

'And so are the cameramen, aren't they?' asked Eric.

'Yes, that's it.'

There were four enormous cameras, each with a cameraman sitting on a high seat looking at the scene through a lens. Some of the cameras were on wheels, and glided silently backwards and forwards, and there was one small camera on a tripod, that did not move.

'But where *is* the producer?' Maddy wanted to know.

'Up there in that little glass box on the wall.'

They looked up. Behind a glass window a number of people seemed to be sitting, looking at a lot of little television monitors.

'May we go up there?' asked Maddy.

'I'll try and take you up,' said Mr Manyweather, 'but it gets awfully crowded there. If the producer comes down on to the floor we'll take the opportunity to slip up.'

'What's that big screen over there?' asked Eric, pointing to something that looked like a magic-lantern screen.

'Oh, that's something I haven't told you about. It's a back-projection screen. A slide, say a picture of some scenery, is projected on to the screen from behind; then the actors play the scene in front of the screen, and when the camera looks at it, it appears just as if the actors really are by the seaside, or in a forest—in fact, against whatever scenery the slide shows. The great advantage is that you can change the scene over and over again, yet only take up the one space in the studio, if you see what I mean. You can also use moving back-projection for moving scenery—out of a train window, or waterfalls, or waves breaking—anything like that, but in that case moving film, not a slide, is thrown on to the screen.'

'Well, I never,' said Maddy. 'What will they think of next? I'd love to see it working.'

As though in answer a slide suddenly flashed on to the screen, showing hills on the horizon and an expanse of sky.

'There, isn't that wonderful!' said Maddy delightedly.

At this moment someone came up and started to chat to Mr Manyweather, and Maddy wandered off behind the screen to see how it worked. There didn't appear to be anything behind the screen except a huge mirror. She made a face at herself in the mirror and did a few ballet steps, then turned to look for the magic-lantern device. Suddenly there seemed to be an extra lot of shouting in the studio, and Mr Manyweather, red-faced, appeared behind the screen.

'Maddy,' he called. 'Come here, they're complaining in the control room about your shadow.'

'My shadow?' repeated Maddy, then when she turned round she understood. Enormous on the screen, right across the sky, was a plumpish silhouette with plaits sticking out at each side.

'Ow, help,' she squeaked, and ran out from behind the screen.

Everyone in the studio was laughing and looking at her. Maddy's face went pink.

'Don't go behind there again,' said the floor manager, although he too was laughing.

'I'll look after her,' promised Mr Manyweather.

Eric also was pink with confusion. 'Don't you dare go away from us again!' he cried. 'You'll get us turned out of the studio if you're not careful.'

'But how did it happen?' whispered Maddy. 'There wasn't a magic-lantern. I went to look. There was only a mirror.'

'Oh dear, oh dear, I didn't explain that because I thought it was too complicated,' said Mr Manyweather. 'The lantern is at the side and throws its beam into the mirror, which reflects it on to the screen. The mirror halves the length of the throw, saving studio space. See?'

Maddy didn't really; all she knew was she'd made a fool of herself.

'I'm awfully sorry,' she said in a small voice.

'It doesn't matter,' said Mr Manyweather. 'It's only a rehearsal. If you'd done it during transmission it would have been a very different matter.'

'Of course, you can't go back and do it again like you can in films,' reflected Maddy.

'No, the performance is being transmitted while it's actually happening.

'That's why so much rehearsal is necessary. Now they're

rehearsing a sketch over there; that'll be more interesting for you. Go over and stand by the side of the set. But *don't* get too close, Maddy.'

Just as Mr Manyweather had told them, the actors in the sketch only spoke in a normal conversational voice, for the mike was suspended over their heads. As they watched, one of the actors dried, and a girl standing near by holding a script prompted him quite loudly.

'Suppose that happened in the programme?' whispered Maddy to Mr Manyweather.

'It wouldn't matter,' he told her. 'The assistant floor manager has a switch on a long cord, and when she presses it, it cuts the sound out while she prompts the actor, and so the viewers don't hear the prompt.'

'I've seen that happen,' said Eric, 'It seems as if the sound on your own set has gone, then it comes back again.'

'That's right,' said Mr Manyweather. 'As long as the actor just stands still and waits for the prompt, and doesn't look agonised, it hardly shows at all.'

Just then came the cry of 'Hold it—hold it, please,' and the floor manager added, 'He's coming down.'

Everyone relaxed and waited for the producer to appear. He came down some steep iron steps into the studio, and went over to the actors taking part in the sketch. 'No, what I mean is this...' he began.

'Now's our chance,' said Mr Manyweather. 'Up we go.'

They went quickly up the stairs into the control room, which was dark and full of cigarette smoke. At first the children could see nothing but the silvery oblongs of the monitors.

'May I just show these two the control room very briefly?' asked Mr Manyweather of an elderly gentleman sitting at a desk in front of the monitors.

'Yes, go ahead. But you'd better clear out when *he* comes back.' The man jerked his head towards the producer down in the studio.

'Sure,' said Mr Manyweather, and as their eyes became accustomed to the darkness, after the bright lights of the studio, he explained to Eric and Maddy who everyone was.

'The girl twiddling the knobs is the vision mixer; the producer sits beside her and tells her which camera he wants transmitted. The producer's secretary sits at his other side, timing the show, and calling out the number of the shot, so that the cameramen and everyone know exactly where they are in the action of the programme. Then, at this other desk, sits the chief engineer, who is in charge of all the technical side of the programme, and the lighting engineer, and the make-up girl and wardrobe assistant. So they, too, can see just how everyone looks on the screen.'

Maddy stared longingly at the vision mixer's panel and wished she could have a go.

'How exactly does it work?' asked Eric.

'Show them, Clare, there's a dear,' said Mr Manyweather.

'Well, I can cut—like this—from one camera to another,' said the girl, pressing a button, so that one picture instantly replaced another on the transmission monitor in front of her. 'Or I can mix—like this.' One picture dissolved slowly into another as she pulled two little levers in opposite directions. 'Or I can fade...' She pulled one lever and the picture faded, leaving a blank screen.

'What fun,' cried Maddy. 'D'you think I could just try it...'

'No,' said Mr Manyweather decidedly. 'You've caused enough trouble already.'

'Is this the young lady who walked across the sky on the B.P.?' asked Clare, laughing. 'I can't tell you how funny it looked from here.'

While they were laughing Mr Manyweather said suddenly, 'Sh. He's coming back. We'd better go.'

They slipped out of the vision control room, into the sound control room, where the 'gram' girl, as Mr Manyweather described her, was putting records on to a long bank of revolving turntables, and a young man was twiddling knobs under another row of monitors.

'He's the sound mixer,' Mr Manyweather told them. 'He does with the sound what the vision mixer does with the pictures.'

Just then the producer strode past them. 'Hullo, old boy,' said Mr Manyweather. 'I've been showing two young visitors over the place; you don't mind, do you...'

'No, no—not at all,' said the producer vaguely, without even looking at them.

'He does look worried,' said Maddy.

'So would I be,' said Mr Manyweather, 'if I'd got to get this show on tonight.'

When they had reached the studio again the floor manager shouted suddenly, 'Break for tea', and instantly the studio became deserted. The lights were switched out, and the cameramen and everybody surged through the doors.

'Well,' said Eric, 'that was quick.'

It gave them a chance to have a close look at some of the equipment. Eric was particularly interested in the cameras, and climbed up on the seat of one of them to look through the lens.

Maddy went on to one of the sets and started singing in what she hoped was an operatic fashion, imitating the soprano who had just been singing.

'For goodness' sake, Maddy,' Mr Manyweather implored her, 'come on, let's go and have some tea, like everyone else.'

They walked through endless corridors and scenery docks to the canteen, where a long queue was curling from the door to the counter.

'Heavens, we'll never get served,' said Mr Manyweather, but Eric and Maddy found it interesting enough just to stand in the queue and look around. Most of the people appeared to be technicians and secretaries, but here and there were splashes of colour where actors and singers and dancers in costume were sitting, drinking tea and chatting. Maddy looked curiously at the costumes—there were ballet dancers, cavaliers, and some children dressed up as birds, their headpieces pushed back on to their shoulders, so that they could eat.

'After tea can we look at the wardrobe and the make-up places?' Maddy asked Mr Manyweather.

'Yes, I'd been planning to take you there.'

At last they collected their tea and a plate of sticky buns, and sat down at a table. All sorts of people kept coming up to talk to Mr Manyweather, and he introduced Maddy and Eric to everybody as 'two young friends'. It was impossible to tell who was what, as they addressed each other by their Christian names.

'That was the assistant controller,' said Mr Manyweather airily, as one gentleman departed.

'And who's that?' asked Eric, indicating a smart young man who looked like a band leader.

'Him? Oh, he's a call-boy.'

Maddy was thrilled to recognise an announcer who had been on the programme that they had watched at Snooks's house.

'Isn't she lovely,' she said. 'She hasn't got much make-up on, has she? It's not a bit like stage or film make-up.'

'No,' agreed Mr Manyweather, 'it's much more delicate. The television cameras see everything in such detail that make-up has to be light—hardly more than a woman wears ordinarily.'

Maddy was so anxious to see the make-up department that she could hardly eat her tea. When they had finished, Mr Manyweather led them down to the basement, into a room lined with mirrors, each surrounded by very bright electric lights. There was a lovely smell of cosmetics, and lots of wigs were arranged on wooden stands shaped like bald heads. Maddy picked one up and perched it on top of her head.

'Look, I'm Little Lord Fauntleroy...'

'Put it down!' cried Eric and Mr Manyweather in one voice.

'Don't touch a thing,' Mr Manyweather said. 'I've got to leave you here for a few minutes, while I go to see the controller. If you touch anything you'll get thrown out. Darling,' he called to a pretty girl in a blue overall, whose name he had obviously forgotten, 'may I leave these two with you for a few minutes? Just let them watch you make up an artiste, will you? They're in the business—two of my schoolchildren.'

'Yes, of course, Leon. Come this way,' said the girl pleasantly to Maddy and Eric.

Under a white cape sat an unidentifiable figure wearing a white turban, and as they watched, the girl began to rub cream into the face.

'Is it going to be a man or a woman?' Maddy demanded loudly.

Eric trod heavily on her toe, and made a fierce face at her. The girl and the figure under the cape both laughed.

'It's a lady,' the make-up girl answered Maddy. And sure enough, when the make-up was finished they recognised a very pretty dancer who had been in the show they had watched rehearsed.

Then Mr Manyweather reappeared, and took them to the wardrobe, where costumes of every description hung on long rails, and men and women in white overalls with needles and thread stuck in their lapels raced about putting in a stitch here and a tuck there, sewing on a ribbon somewhere else. 'Isn't it lovely!' cried Maddy, sniffing the smell of clothes being pressed.

'We mustn't stay, they're so busy,' said Mr Manyweather. 'Although most of the costumes are hired, they do make a considerable number themselves, and there are always several shows in rehearsal at once, all needing attention.'

'Where can we go now?' demanded Maddy as they went out into the corridor again.

'Well, you haven't seen everything by a long chalk,' said Mr Manyweather, 'but I'm afraid it's all for today, because I've got to dash off.'

As they climbed into 'Agatha' Eric said, 'Thanks most awfully, Mr Manyweather. It's been jolly interesting.'

'Rather,' said Maddy as 'Agatha' started up with a series of explosions. 'I've quite decided I don't want to act in the theatre or on the films. I want to be in television.'

4

MRS BOSHAM

One day, in the fifth week of term, Rosalind rushed into the 'Babies' classroom crying, 'What do you think? Glorious news—I've just seen Mrs Seymore, and she says that Mr Whitfield's buying a television set—to go in the common room—it's being installed tomorrow, and anyone will be able to watch it.'

'How heavenly! Wizard!' came glad cries from all those who had not sets at home.

'Anyone will be able to watch—even us?' asked Maddy suspiciously.

They were used to the 'Babies' being excluded from certain activities on the grounds that they were 'not old enough'.

'Well—Mrs Seymore said we could watch in the afternoons sometimes. I don't know whether that means we can't in the evenings.'

When the 'Babies' told him about the set Mr Manyweather was delighted to hear the news.

'Now, don't just sit in front of it like a lot of morons, letting it lap over you. You must watch from a professional point of view. Consider the technique of the acting—see who you think is good and who isn't, and why.'

Every day as soon as lessons were over, the 'Babies' assembled in the common room and watched the children's programme. Then Maddy and Zillah would fly back to Fitzherbert Street for their evening meal, and back again to the Academy, where there were always some seniors watching—generally a play they particularly wanted to see, or a programme in which a friend was appearing. Maddy and Zillah would creep into the darkened room and curl up on the floor, and stay there until it was so late that even Mrs Bosham's conscience was uneasy about them. When their eyes were smarting and their backs aching, they would slip out very quietly, for they were still not quite sure that the juniors were allowed to watch after the children's programme was over.

Drinking cocoa in Mrs Bosham's basement, Maddy would tell her all that they had just seen, while Mrs Bosham interjected cries of 'Well, I never' and 'She *didn't!*'

And every evening the conversation finished on the same line.

'It's no good, I'll have to get a telly on the never-never.'

The effect of Mr Manyweather's television lessons on the acting of the Academy was most marked. At first the other instructors were distraught because in their classes all the students were underacting and using too little voice. 'You'll never fill a theatre with *that* voice,' cried Mrs Seymore in despair. 'Too small—it's all too small,' stormed Mr Whitfield, after the top class had done their first public performance of the term. The seniors who were in their last year had to put on a play every three weeks, to accustom them to the rate of work outside in the professional world.

Poor Mr Manyweather began to feel quite worried.

'They're all blaming me,' he said to Maddy's class, 'because you can't keep to two separate techniques. You've got to learn to be able to switch over. You mustn't ruin your chances for the theatre just because you hope to act on television. It's ridiculous.'

So Mr Manyweather would keep saying in his lessons, 'Show me how you'd do it for the theatre,' then, 'and now, for television.'

He arrived one day carrying some parcels even bulkier than usual. These when unwrapped turned out to contain large, rough models of television cameras. 'Mock-ups' of cameras he called them.

These mock-ups were fixed on to the backs of chairs and pushed about the room, to give the students the feeling of playing to different cameras all the time. There was quite a lot of competition among the boys to be 'cameramen'.

'Ooh, I've got a lovely close-up of Maddy,' Colin would cry, looking through the imitation lens. 'She does look funny...'

This did a great deal to make them less conscious of the cameras.

'It's to give you a sense of television,' Mr Manyweather was always telling them. 'I want you to be conscious of the camera, but not camera-conscious, if you see what I mean. A good television actor knows exactly which camera's taking him at any given moment, and how long the shot is. He knows he's got to *give* more on the long shot than in the close-ups, but he never lets the viewer suspect for a moment that there's even a camera in sight.'

The television mania swept the whole Academy. The 'Babies' even enjoyed the advertisement spots on commercial television, and played at acting them individually, but leaving out the name of the product for the others to guess. The seniors were allowed to plan whole television productions, with one of the students as producer, and Mr Manyweather watched them and criticised them as seriously as if they were the real thing.

Every week the two best pupils in the 'Babies' television class were taken to the studios to watch a rehearsal, and Mr Manyweather managed to arrange matters so that a different couple came top each week. Poor Zillah was still so nervous that she never got through a speech without drying, but one day he said to her, 'Well, you know, that was so sincere—at least the bit you remembered was—and you looked so enchanting that I think the viewers might forgive the dries, so you'd better come on Saturday and bring Armand with you.'

Armand was a French boy, who spoke very little English; his father was in the diplomatic service, and had just been posted to London. Armand had no ambition to become an actor, but his parents thought that more attention would be paid to his speech at the Academy than at an ordinary school. He was hampered by his lack of English to such a degree that he lagged behind in all subjects except French, where, of course, his accent put everyone else to shame.

'What with Zillah's accent and Armand's, they'll wonder at the studios what the Academy's coming to,' Snooks giggled to Maddy.

'We can't all be Cockneys,' Maddy crushed her as usual.

Zillah came back marvelling at the many wonders of the television studio, and as anxious as everyone else to do some acting on the small screen.

During the following week some free seats were sent to the Academy for a commercial television quiz programme, which was to be televised with a live audience from a theatre in South London. A certain number of tickets were allotted to each class, and Zillah and Maddy were both fortunate enough to be given one. Each ticket admitted two people to the show, but anyone under seventeen had to be accompanied by an adult.

'Bags I Mrs Bosham,' cried Maddy.

'But—but then I shan't have a grown-up,' wailed Zillah.

'Well,' Maddy racked her brains, 'there's Mr Manyweather—or Mrs Seymore,' she added doubtfully.

'I could never ask *them*,' cried Zillah.

'Well then, ask one of the seniors who's over seventeen,' said Maddy.

'Oh, I daren't.'

'I'll find someone for you,' promised Maddy, 'even if I have to stop and ask a passer-by in the street.'

'No, no,' cried Zillah, terrified that Maddy might do as she threatened.

But in the end Snooks came to the rescue.

'You can have my father,' she offered largely. 'Both my parents want to come, so he'll be glad to share your ticket.'

Mrs Bosham, too, was thrilled with the idea. She couldn't quite gather what it was they were going to do, but knew it was something to do with the 'telly', and that it would make an outing. She deliberated at length on which hat she should wear, until Maddy had to assure her that she wouldn't necessarily be *seen* by the cameras.

'Of course, they do sometimes show a few of the people in the audience,' Maddy admitted. 'But not very often.'

'Still, there's your friend's Mum and Dad to think about,' went on Mrs Bosham. 'We don't want to let *them* down, do we?'

Maddy was sure that Mrs Snooks would be horrified by Mrs Bosham's hat, but she didn't really care. It was so exciting to be going to a real television show, of a type so different from the one she had watched before.

They arranged to meet outside the theatre, and Maddy and Zillah and Mrs Bosham were there in good time.

When the Snooks family turned up Maddy thought that Mrs Snooks's hat was just as ridiculous as Mrs Bosham's, only obviously more expensive. They all jabbered excitedly and then made their way into the theatre, with a stream of other people.

It was a beautiful old theatre that had been a music hall until it had been bought by the commercial television company. Outside it was rather shabby, but inside it was very ornate and had been redecorated; the gilded and scrolled balconies gleamed, and the red plush seats had been newly upholstered.

'Isn't it beautiful?' breathed Maddy.

'Is this a theatre?' asked Zillah. 'I like it better than the cinemas.'

Of course everyone laughed at this, but it seemed terrible to think that Zillah's first visit to a real theatre was to see a television show.

The television cameras were placed at various vantage points in the theatre, one of them being on a ramp running down the centre of the auditorium. 'I do hope our seats aren't directly behind the camera,' said Mrs Snooks, 'or we shan't see anything.'

But they found themselves in quite good seats slightly to one side, so that, despite the camera, they could see the whole of the stage.

In the auditorium there were a lot of people from the Academy to wave to and this kept Maddy and Snooks busy until the orchestra struck up. The lights in the theatre were not dimmed at all, which seemed strange. Then the compère came in front of the stage curtains and told them that there was still some time to go before they would be on the air, and so he would tell them what was going to take place. He had a plug microphone on a long flex, so that he was able to walk down the steps from the stage and up and down the gangways of the auditorium.

'Now, we'll just have a little rehearsal with some test questions,' he said. 'And the first person to shout out the answer will receive a prize.'

The questions were very easy, and the prizes were quite small—but with each winner the compère exchanged a few words, and to some he said, 'And would you like to come up on the stage and compete for the big prizes while we're on the air?'

As the audience warmed up, the questions became a little more difficult. After the question, 'What lady was urged in a song to raise her lower limbs?' there was a momentary pause, then Mrs Bosham suddenly screeched 'Mother Brown' so loudly that people near her almost jumped out of their seats.

'That's right—Mother Brown it is. Give her a prize.'

The very beautiful girl in evening dress who was the compère's assistant presented Mrs Bosham with a box of soap and talcum powder.

'Now, madam, what is your name?' asked the compère, leaning over and holding the mike close to her mouth.

'Bosham—Mrs Bosham.'

'And you're—a Londoner, I think.'

'Oh, yerse—born and bred...'

Mrs Bosham was scarlet in the face with excitement, which made her look even fatter than usual. Maddy and Zillah were doubled up with giggles.

'And—er—you're a housewife?'

'Well, I'm a widow woman, as you might say. And I takes in lodgers.'

For some reason this appealed to the audience and they applauded.

'Now, this song—"Knees up, Mother Brown"—you're a Londoner, so you ought to know it. D'you think you could sing the chorus?'

'Ooh,' squealed Mrs Bosham, 'I couldn't—really I couldn't...'

'Go on,' hissed Maddy and Snooks.

'Well, I'll 'ave a go at it.'

Mrs Bosham's voice was not melodious, but it was certainly penetrating, and the audience applauded loudly.

'Now, Mrs Cosham...'

'Bosham, please,' she corrected the compère.

'Oh, yes—Mrs Bosham—when we go on the air, in a few minutes' time, will you join us on the stage and enter for the quiz competition? There are some magnificent prizes you can win—a washing machine, a radiogram, a television set...'

'Righto,' said Mrs Bosham promptly.

'Jolly good. Now please give your name and address to my assistant.'

The compère passed on to find more victims, and the beautiful young lady wrote down Mrs Bosham's name and address and showed her a list of various subjects from which she could choose one, on which to answer questions.

'What about cookery?' asked the young lady tactfully. 'That's quite a good subject, don't you think?'

'No, no,' Maddy urged Mrs Bosham, throwing tact to the winds. 'Don't choose cookery.'

'Well—er—current events then?'

'No—I don't think I'd know them.'

The assistant looked at her doubtfully. 'Well, what about Old London?' she said at last in desperation.

'Old London—yes, that's a good 'un,' agreed Mrs Bosham. 'Don't expect I'll know any of the answers though.'

'Oh, yes you will; they'll be quite simple questions. Now, would you care to follow me, and come through behind the stage so that you're ready when it's your turn.'

With a great flurry Mrs Bosham departed, giggling and squealing.

'Oh, I *do* hope she wins something.' Maddy was bouncing up and down with excitement.

'And—and will everyone watching at home see Mrs Bosham?' asked Zillah wonderingly.

'Yes, of course,' said Maddy.

'Well, it will be a real treat for them,' said Mr Snooks sincerely, and Maddy came to the conclusion that he was really a very nice man indeed.

Before the televised part of the programme started, there was an air of excitement over the whole theatre. The cameramen, perched on their cameras, were preparing to go into action in earnest.

Just when they went on the air the compère told a funny story so that everyone was laughing as the curtain went up, and the programme had begun.

Maddy and her party were on such tenterhooks, waiting for Mrs Bosham's entrance, that they hardly noticed the first part of the programme. A very clever young man, who was an Oxford undergraduate, answered some mathematical questions and won an electric razor. A rather silly girl didn't know any of the answers to some questions about the theatre, and a housewife won a washing machine for giving the correct replies to the cookery questions. Then came the break in the programme while the advertisements were on, and during this time the compère told another funny story, so that the audience were all laughing when they were seen again. And then it was Mrs Bosham's turn.

Maddy and Zillah and Snooks were giggling and nudging each other, and were so restless that the people in the row behind protested.

'And now,' said the compère, 'we come to our next contestant—a Londoner born and bred. Mrs Bosham,' he announced with a flourish. There was a roar of applause, and Mrs Bosham waddled on to the stage, beaming with confusion. The compère put his arm round her, and drew her to stand as near as possible to him.

'That's to let the camera get a nice close two-shot,' said Maddy knowledgeably.

'Now then, Mrs Bosham, how long have you lived in London?'

'All me life. Sixty years—getting on fer...'

'Sixty years—and so you feel you're qualified to answer questions about Old London?'

'Well, I'll do me best—can't do more, as I always say.'

'That's the spirit. Well now, here in a sealed envelope are the questions on Old London. Nobody has seen them since they were put there by the university professor who sets the questions. There are three questions. If you can answer all of them, you'll get one of our mammoth prizes. If you can only answer two, you'll get a smaller prize. If you can only answer one, you'll get a consolation prize, and if you can't answer any—well—I'll give you a great big kiss!'

Mrs Bosham screeched delightedly.

'Now, I will open the envelope.'

He did so with a flourish.

'And here are the questions. Now then—first question. Where did the old Shaftesbury Theatre stand?'

'*Where?*' said Mrs Bosham. 'Why, Shaftesbury Avenue, of course.'

'That is *correct*.'

The compère led the applause, as though she had just answered a very difficult question.

'You've got a consolation prize anyhow, even if you don't know any more of the answers. Now then, the second question. Name three famous music halls that are no longer in use as such.'

'Well now,' said Mrs Bosham, 'there's the Empire; that's a picture 'ouse now; and the 'Olborn, and—and...'

She floundered. Maddy was nearly going mad.

'Go on—go on,' she shouted.

'Do *you* know any more?' asked Snooks.

'No, no, but *she* must...'

'Oh, yerse—of course.' Light dawned slowly on Mrs Bosham's large countenance. 'There's this 'ere one—the Royal. Now it's bin bought by these 'ere telly people.'

There were roars of laughter and applause.

'First class, Mrs Bosham! You've got a nice prize anyhow, even if you don't get the next answer. And if you *do* get it—let's have a look at the prizes you will be able to choose from...'

Some curtains at the back of the stage parted, and revealed an imposing array of refrigerators, radiograms and television sets.

'Now then, which have you got your eye on?' demanded the compère.

'Oh, I'd have the telly.'

'Oh, you would, would you? Now can you tell me why?'

'Well, fer me lodgers.'

'There now, isn't that a grand idea?' said the compère fulsomely, as the curtains swung together again.

'Now, all you've got to do is answer one more question and you'll win that handsome television cabinet. And here is the last question. Where did the Great Exhibition of London take place—and what happened to the building in which it took place? It's a difficult one, and you've got to get both parts. Now think carefully. No hints from the audience, please. If she thinks carefully the answer will be crystal clear.'

There was laughter from the audience at this hint, but it did not seem to sink into Mrs Bosham's brain.

'Well now, it was a little before my time,' she began cautiously, and had to wait for the audience to stop laughing. 'But that exhibition was held in the Crystal Palace. Oh, I see—crystal clear—thanks fer the 'int.'

'Crystal Palace is correct. Now you've only got the second half of the question to answer. What became of the Crystal Palace?'

'Well, it was moved from Hyde Park—that's where it *was*, you see, and then it was burnt down, after it was moved to—well Crystal Palace, they call it...'

'Yes, but where *is* the place that's now called Crystal Palace? Can you answer that, Mrs Bosham?'

There was a tense silence while she thought. 'Well, it's—it's South London somewhere, somewhere round...'

'Near Sydenham,' said Snooks under her breath, trying to mesmerise Mrs Bosham into getting it.

'No,' said Mrs Bosham. 'No, I can't say I know.'

There was a groan from the audience. Suddenly she brightened.

''Ere young man, read that question again.'

He did so.

'It's not in the question. All it asks is what became of it. Well, I've told you—burnt down.'

'You're right, Mrs Bosham. Quite right,' admitted the compère. 'Take your television set—you deserve it.'

Maddy and Zillah went nearly crazy with joy, as Mrs Bosham gave the compère two resounding kisses, one on each cheek.

'Good old Mrs Bosham,' said Snooks. 'There now, aren't you lucky, Maddy? You've got a television to watch, after all, without having to go to the Academy all the time.'

Mrs Bosham returned to her seat, almost collapsing with excitement. She had to open her massive handbag and bring out a large handkerchief with which to mop her face, and then a bottle of smelling salts with which to revive herself.

'Well, just fancy,' was all she could say, while the others congratulated her and thumped her on the back.

'Fancy you knowing all those things,' Maddy marvelled.

'I never *knew* I knew them,' Mrs Bosham protested modestly.

The rest of the show did not seem particularly interesting after all the intense excitement they had had, and they kept plying Mrs Bosham with whispered questions.

'When will it come?' Maddy wanted to know.

'Tomorrow or the next day.'

'How exciting.'

'What's it like backstage?' Snooks asked.

'Untidy,' was Mrs Bosham's reply.

'All the excitement has made me ravenous,' said Maddy when the show was over and they were filing out.

'Let's go and have something to eat, then,' said Mr Snooks, confirming Maddy's opinion that he was a very nice man.

As they went out of the theatre people kept coming up to Mrs Bosham and congratulating her, and telling her she was 'as good as a tonic', and making other complimentary remarks.

'It's bin the most exciting day I've 'ad since the Coronation,' she said as they came out into the fresh air.

'Now,' said Mr Snooks, 'where shall we eat?'

It was difficult to find anywhere suitable, as there seemed to be nothing but snack bars and public houses.

'Oh, look,' said Maddy. 'Fish and Chip Bar.'

'I've never been in a fish and chip bar,' said Mrs Snooks. 'It might be fun.'

'Nor have I,' said Zillah.

'You've never been in a fish and chip shop?' cried Mrs Bosham, as horrified as the others had been at hearing Zillah had never been to a theatre.

They went upstairs to the 'dining-room', and there on long marble-topped tables that reminded Maddy of an old-fashioned washstand in the attic at her grannie's, they ate enormous platefuls of fish, cooked in bright orange batter, and piles of golden chips.

'This occasion must be celebrated,' said Mr Snooks, and called for glasses of bright-red fizzy raspberryade, in which to drink Mrs Bosham's health.

'Now where do you think I should *put* the telly?' pondered Mrs Bosham. 'In the droring-room, or in the basement?' The 'droring-room' was hardly ever used by the lodgers, for it was very cold, and furnished with hideous heavy furniture, and had lace curtains that were rarely washed and gave the room a musty smell.

'Oh, in the basement,' cried Maddy. 'It's so much cosier. And if you put it in the drawing-room all the lodgers would watch it, but if you have it in your basement they will have to wait to be invited.'

'Course I could put it in the dining-room—but no, we'd never get meals over.'

Mrs Bosham toyed with the thought of the television for a long time, until the Snooks family suddenly realised that they would lose their last train if they did not hurry. Everybody thanked everyone else for a lovely evening, and Mr Snooks insisted on paying the bill. Then they went out into the dark street, and the girls shouted goodnights to each other as they went their opposite ways.

Next day was Friday, and Maddy was dying to tell Mr Manyweather all about the previous night's outing, but when he arrived he, too, was bursting with news. His hair was untidier than ever, and behind his thick spectacles his eyes were gleaming with excitement. He sat down at the piano and struck a thunderous chord in order to gain the attention of the class.

'Now,' he said, 'I must have a careful look at you.'

He got up and went round the whole class peering short-sightedly at them, stroking his chin and saying 'M'm'. This made them all giggle, and he had to strike another chord in order to quieten them.

'Oh, what's the matter, Mr Manyweather?' cried Rosalind. 'Do tell us.'

'Well, it's all rather exciting,' said Mr Manyweather. 'A friend of mine who produces for commercial television is looking for a girl or a boy to take part in a series for children, and he's holding auditions next week. He knows I teach here, so he asked me if I had any pupils who might do, and, if so, to send them along. The age limits are over twelve and under fifteen. Now, that cuts some of you out, doesn't it?'

It did. It eliminated Rosalind, Zillah and Armand, who all groaned loudly.

'Television experience, while not absolutely essential, would be a help. That puts Buster and Snooks well in the running. And a blond would be preferred—Maddy, here's your chance—or Colin...'

Everybody giggled at the idea of Colin being called a blond. His hair was straw-coloured and he had eyelashes to match.

'I think all of you who come into the age group might as well go out for it,' continued Mr Manyweather. 'But I warn you that none of you may meet their requirements. There'll be hundreds going in for the job, and it would be a feather in our caps if someone from the Academy got it.'

There was an excited buzz of conversation as people discussed their chances, and the three who were too old bemoaned their fate.

'What sort of things have we got to do for the audition, Mr Manyweather?' asked Buster.

'A short speech of your own choice, and then they'll give you things to do on sight.'

Everybody groaned. Although they had plenty of practice at sight-reading they all dreaded it.

'What studios do we have to go to?' asked Colin eagerly.

'Not to any studios. Just to the producer's office.'

'However will he get a hundred into his office?' Maddy wanted to know.

'Not all at once, Gretchen. You will each have separate appointments. Now, I'll make a list of all your names and give it to him. After that we'll consider you individually and

77

decide what each shall do for the audition. And as Zillah and Rosalind and Armand are too old they can come and sit up at the table with me and be an advisory panel, helping me to decide.'

This was the sort of suggestion that made Mr Manyweather popular. He never let anyone feel out of things.

The rest of the lesson was spent hearing speeches and discussing what would be best for whom.

That afternoon on the way back to Fitzherbert Street Maddy said, 'I'm awfully glad you're not going to the audition, Zillah.'

'You selfish thing...'

'No, what I mean is, I'm glad I haven't got to compete against you. You see, I intend to win this audition!'

5

MORGAN EVANS

As Maddy and Mrs Bosham walked up Kingsway in the hot sunshine Maddy felt more nervous about the audition than she had ever felt about anything before. The trouble was that she wanted so desperately to get the job. Since Mrs Bosham's television set had arrived Maddy had spent hours sitting in front of it, telling herself that she could do just as well as any of the girls of her own age who took part in programmes.

'Your trouble is, you've got too much bounce,' Mr Manyweather had told her. 'It's an unusual thing to have to tell anyone, but you have so much vivacity that you would appear to be about to pop out through the screen and bite people.'

The class had roared with laughter at this description of Maddy. She had laughed too, but had determined to get her audition speech really beautifully under control. Mr Manyweather had warned them that it would be wise to do the speeches of youthful characters, not of adults. Usually the

79

Academy encouraged even the 'Babies' to do classical speeches for auditions, however much too adult they might seem for young students, but on this occasion Mr Manyweather advised Maddy to find something quite childish. She had taken him literally at first, and had found a revolting little poem in baby language entitled 'I'se Not Cwying', with which she reduced the class to helpless laughter, and Mr Manyweather to shudders of agony.

'That was without exception the most nauseating exhibition I've ever seen,' he said, wiping his spectacles as she finished. 'Don't you dare repeat it at the audition. I'd rather you did Lady Macbeth.'

Eventually he found for her a speech of Gerda's from *The Snow Queen*, which was quite dramatic but was the right age, and told her, 'Work on it—it needs all the sincerity in the world. I'm sorry I shan't have an opportunity to hear you again before you go for the audition. Your day is Thursday, Thursday morning at eleven-fifteen. You ought to have a chaperone with you. Can your mother go?'

'No,' said Maddy. 'She's miles away in Fenchester, but I expect Mrs Bosham would like to come. She's my landlady.'

Mrs Bosham was only too pleased to oblige.

'The 'ousework can go to pot fer once,' she said. 'I'd love to come to one of them there studios and see what 'appens.'

'It won't be a proper studio,' Maddy warned her, 'just the producer's office. The producer's name is Morgan Evans. He's Welsh,' she added unnecessarily.

She had not gone to the Academy at all that morning, but had spent a long time brushing her hair and dressing very carefully. Now, in a neat blue dress with a clean white collar, and navy shoes and white socks, she looked as neat as a bandbox, walking along beside Mrs Bosham.

'You do me credit today,' Mrs Bosham told her.

Maddy was unusually quiet, as she was wondering about Morgan Evans, and whether he would be very Welsh—like Fluellen in *Henry V*.

'I reckon that's the place,' said Mrs Bosham suddenly, pointing to an enormous building that towered up over Kingsway. They stood still and looked up at it, and then went in. Inside there was confusion. People were surging about as though they had trains to catch, builders were hammering, and the array of telephones on the commissionaire's desk rang continuously.

'I have an appointment to see Mr Morgan Evans,' said Maddy importantly to the uniformed commissionaire behind the desk. 'It is for eleven-fifteen. We're a little early, I'm afraid.'

'Better too early than too late, I always say,' Mrs Bosham chimed in, and the commissionaire looked at her curiously.

'I'll just find out if Mr Evans is ready to see you, miss,' said the man, picking up a phone. 'What name is it?'

'Madeleine Fayne,' said Maddy.

He consulted a list of extensions then plugged in and rang a number.

'Mr Morgan Evans there?' he inquired a few moments later. Maddy could hear a voice squeaking rather crossly at the other end. The commissionaire sighed, said, 'Thanks', and put the phone down.

'Seems to 've moved. Have to try again.'

'This is a madhouse,' the commissionaire confided to Maddy and Mrs Bosham. 'Nobody seems to stay in the same office for two minutes. Like musical chairs, it is. Got the builders in, y'see.'

At last the producer was tracked down, and by this time it was well past eleven-fifteen.

'Right, Mr Evans, I'll send them up,' said the commissionaire. 'Third floor, turn right, number three-six-two,' he told Maddy.

Mrs Bosham was a trifle doubtful about the lift. 'But there's no one to work it,' she objected.

'It's automatic,' Maddy told her.

'Maybe it is and maybe it isn't,' said Mrs Bosham, shaking her head. 'You'll not get me in a contraption like that. Silly 'aporths we'd look if it got stuck. Stairs are good enough fer me. Come on.'

By the time they reached the third floor they were out of breath and panting.

'I can't go in yet,' gasped Maddy. 'Wait a minute till I get my breath back.'

They stood still in the middle of the corridor, and let the stream of messengers and secretaries and technicians swirl past them. An office door, marked 362, stared them in the face. Suddenly the door opened and a girl looked out. 'Oh, are you Madeleine Fayne?' she asked.

'Yes,' said Maddy, who had regained her breath.

'Oh, good, we thought you'd got lost on the way up. Come in. Are you Mrs Fayne?' she inquired of Mrs Bosham.

'Oh, no, no—I'm Mrs Bosham.'

'Oh, I *see*,' said the girl, as though that explained everything.

The office was very small indeed, and squashed inside it were three desks, littered with papers and books and files. The walls were covered with photographs of actors and actresses, and the room seemed to be filled with people. A middle-aged man, with thick hair that was beginning to go grey, sat at the largest of the desks, and was looking piercingly at Maddy with extremely blue eyes from under heavy brows.

'This is Mr Morgan Evans and this is his assistant,' the girl said, and proceeded to sit down at a desk with a typewriter.

The assistant was sitting at a small desk with two telephones on it, and two other young men were sitting on the floor, writing furiously on foolscap, clipped on to script boards.

'This is Madeleine Fayne and chaperone,' the girl reminded Mr Morgan Evans.

The assistant found a very small and rather rickety chair for Mrs Bosham, and she sat down on it gingerly.

'Well, Madeleine, how old are you?'

'Fourteen,' said Maddy.

'H'm—and you are one of Leon Manyweather's protégées, aren't you?'

'Yes, that's right.'

'H'm—I've heard something about you. Let's see, you've not done any television, have you?'

'No,' said Maddy. 'But I was in a film.'

'Ah, yes.' Mr Evans narrowed his eyes. 'I thought I'd seen you somewhere before. An historical film, wasn't it?'

'Yes. It was called *Forsaken Crown*.'

'H'm. You played the lead, the heroine, didn't you?'

'Yes.'

'H'm—it was quite a long and difficult part. Are you doing any more films?'

'Not at present. My parents want me to complete my training at the Academy first. But television wouldn't interfere with that, would it?'

'Television interferes with everything,' said Mr Morgan Evans gloomily, and everyone in the office laughed. 'I won't go into details about what we're wanting until I've seen what you can do. It's not so much an actress we need as a personality. The job really calls for someone with a lot of experience, but who looks very young.'

Maddy nearly decided to change her mind and do 'I'se Not Cwying' after all, but then didn't dare, because Mr Manyweather had condemned it so definitely.

'Have you had any stage experience?'

'In repertory, in my home town.'

'H'm.'

Everybody looked at Maddy very hard, weighing her up, and she looked right back at them, determined not to show that she was nervous.

'Right. Well, let's hear your audition. Stand over there by the door.'

It was the only corner of the room where there were a few square inches to spare.

Maddy took up the position in which she had been taught to stand—not too stiff, nice and relaxed, with one foot slightly in front of the other. Then she reminded herself not to over-act, and tried to imagine that just her head was framed in a television close-up. All was going beautifully, and she knew she was being quite sincere, yet not being too carried away, when something terrible happened. Mrs Bosham's chair collapsed. She landed on the floor with a screech of horror among the splintered pieces of wood. There was general confusion, and everyone tried not to laugh while she was helped to her feet. The assistant gave up his chair, a much stronger one, and she was settled into it, very red in the face.

'Start again, dear,' said Morgan Evans.

Maddy did so. But when she reached the particular passage during which Mrs Bosham's downfall had taken place, she suddenly remembered it, and felt a giggle bubbling up inside her. She tried to quell it, but first of all a terribly unsuitable grin appeared on her face, then her voice broke, and she collapsed altogether, bending double and holding her tummy.

'Oh, I'm sorry—oh, I'm sorry,' she kept exclaiming between paroxysms. Her laughter was so infectious that everyone joined in, including Mrs Bosham.

'I'm that sorry,' said Mrs Bosham, wiping her streaming eyes. 'It's all my fault. She'd be all right if it 'adn't been fer me.'

'Look, I think it'll take some time for us to settle down again, don't you, Maddy? So we'll go and have a coffee, and then try again. What you have done so far is very good indeed.'

They all adjourned to the restaurant behind the building, and while they drank coffee Morgan Evans pumped Maddy about herself, and seemed surprised and amused by her answers.

'Now, I'll tell you what it's all about. Have you ever heard of a magazine called *The World of Youth*?'

'Oh, yes, it's for children, isn't it? Well, teenagers.'

'That's right. Well, this magazine is having a half-hour programme every weekend, intended to appeal to girls and boys in their teens, and based on the sort of things they have in their magazine. Now, they want someone to compère the programme—it can be either a girl or a boy—they don't care which—but it's got to be someone with a lot of poise, a lot of acting ability and complete self assurance.'

'Sounds just like me,' said Maddy, giggling.

'But it'll be hard work. It'll mean mid-week rehearsals, and then all day Saturday for about fourteen weeks.'

'Sounds wonderful,' said Maddy longingly. 'Would I be able to miss any lessons?'

'I'm afraid not,' laughed Morgan Evans. 'The rehearsals would be arranged so that you *didn't* miss any schooling.'

'Pity,' said Maddy. 'Oh, I do hope I can do it...'

'We're auditioning hundreds of youngsters,' said Morgan Evans. 'Before we finally decide we'll probably hold a camera audition.'

'How exciting,' said Maddy. 'I have been inside a television studio, you know.'

And she proceeded to describe their outing with Mr Manyweather.

By the time they had finished coffee Maddy was feeling much more confident; Mrs Bosham had recovered her composure, and was talking sixteen to the dozen to the secretary, who was listening in a somewhat dazed fashion.

'Well, back to the salt mines,' said Morgan Evans, and they all trailed back to the office.

'I don't think I'll ask you to render the same passage again, Maddy, in case we all get afflicted in the same way a second time,' said the producer. 'Instead, I'll give you something to read.'

'Oh, help,' said Maddy. 'I'm not too good at sight reading.'

'Nobody is, but you'd be working at such speed in this series that if you were a bad reader at rehearsal it would hold up everyone else.'

He handed her a script. 'Now take a look at this. Read it over to yourself for a few minutes, and then read Helen's part to me.'

Maddy took the script and began to read it rather fearfully to herself. It seemed to be a commentary on a trip to Cornwall. Helen's lines described the journey, but other characters kept butting in all the time, and Maddy got confused as to what was happening. 'You do want me just to read Helen, don't you?' she asked.

'Yes, skip the other people's lines.'

As she read, the phone kept ringing, but the secretary answered it in as soft a voice as possible, and the other people all kept silent in order not to interrupt Maddy's study.

'Right?' said Mr Morgan Evans at last. 'Let's have it then.'

Maddy knew that she was reading very badly, but the layout of the script was confusing. It was quite unlike an ordinary play. The dialogue was in a column at the right side of the page, and a description of the action was in another column at the left side. Mr Manyweather had shown them such a script at the studios, and had promised to try and bring some for them to rehearse with him, but had not been able to do so.

When she had finished Maddy said shamefacedly, 'Oh dear, that wasn't very good.'

'It wasn't too bad,' said Mr Morgan Evans. 'Quite a lot of the children we've seen just couldn't read it at all. In fact, I began to wonder if some of them *could* read. But you see, you'd have a great deal of that sort of material to cope with. Do you think you could mange it?'

'Oh, yes,' said Maddy fervently. 'I'm absolutely sure I could.'

'Right. Well, we've got dozens more to see—but you never know. Now, if you'll give my secretary your address and phone number we'll know where to contact you. Or it might be done through Leon Manyweather. By the way, do you think your parents would object to you doing this?'

'Oh, no,' said Maddy airily. 'They're used to anything.'

'Good. Well, you may be hearing from us.'

Maddy said goodbye all round, and so did Mrs Bosham, who added, 'I'm that sorry about the chair.'

In silence they made their way down the stairs, and Maddy did not speak until they were out in the street.

'Well now, I wonder...' she said.

'I think you done very well,' said Mrs Bosham. 'Course, me and that chair was a bit of a bloomer—I'm ever so sorry. And you were just doing your piece real nice. Still, it gave you a chance to 'ave a nice talk to the gentleman, while we was 'aving coffee.'

'Yes,' Maddy agreed. 'But I didn't read very well. It was a jolly difficult piece. Oh, I don't think I've got the job.'

And yet they had seemed to like her. The way they had all looked at her, in a careful, calculating sort of way, had made her feel there was a chance.

'I should try and forget about it now, ducks,' advised Mrs Bosham. 'Then if anything *does* happen about it, it'll come as a nice surprise.'

It was easy to talk about forgetting, but not so easy to do it, for at the Academy everyone was talking about the auditions. When Maddy went into the canteen for lunch she was swooped on by Buster and Snooks, who had not yet had their auditions, and was made to tell them all about it.

'Sounds to me as if you've got the job,' said Buster gloomily. 'Having coffee and everything.'

'But that was only because Mrs Bosham's chair collapsed,' said Maddy.

'Is he *nice?*' Snooks demanded.

'Yes, terribly nice. Not funny, like Mr Manyweather. But nice.'

The other two girls were going for their auditions the following morning, Buster a quarter of an hour before Snooks, and Mrs Snooks was taking them both. Eric and Colin were going in the afternoon, so it was totally impossible for Maddy to put the audition out of her mind, either at school or afterwards, when she kept going over and over the interview to Zillah and saying, 'What do you think?'

Zillah did not know what to think, as she had never been to an audition in her life. That evening every time the phone rang at Fitzherbert Street Maddy rushed to answer it, but it was always either a wrong number or a call for one of the other lodgers.

The next day was Friday, and during the television lesson everyone who had already been to the audition told Mr Manyweather about it in detail. He listened in an interested fashion, and when they had finished he said, 'It sounds as if you all did quite nicely, but you can't *all* get it. In fact none of you may; someone from quite another school may be the lucky one. But whatever the result, it is good experience for you to have been up for the audition. You'll all go up for many an audition that you don't get. You realise that, don't you?'

Maddy told herself that of course she knew it. But she had always been so lucky about things...

Just then Buster and Snooks burst in, having returned from their auditions, and they, too, had to tell their experiences in detail.

'That only leaves Eric and Colin to go this afternoon, doesn't it?' said Mr Manyweather. 'Well, I don't suppose we'll hear the result until next week, and now we must get on with some work.'

But just then the bell rang for the end of the period, so they didn't.

For several days nothing was heard about the results of the audition. Every morning the 'Babies' demanded accusingly of each other, 'Heard anything?' only to be told, 'No, not a murmur.'

Then one afternoon as they sat at lessons in the schoolhouse the door opened and Miss Smith, the secretary of the Academy, came in. She was a smart, brisk woman with kindly eyes, who always took a deep interest in the fortunes of all students and ex-students.

'Maddy,' she said, after apologising for the interruption to the geography teacher, who was drawing a map on the blackboard, 'Maddy, you're wanted outside.'

'*Wanted?*' exclaimed Maddy. 'I haven't done anything...'

'Not that sort of wanted. Will you excuse her a moment? It's rather important.'

Outside in the corridor stood Mr Manyweather, looking pleased and excited.

'Gretchen, my girl,' he said, 'they want you for a camera audition. That's good, isn't it?'

Maddy executed a few steps of the can-can to express her delight.

'Mind you, it doesn't mean you've got it. But Morgan Evans seemed very pleased with you. And what's even better—the camera audition is going to be in the form of a panel game. Now, you're better value when you're being spontaneous than when you've learned up a party piece, so I think your chances are good.'

'Is anyone else going from here?' Maddy wanted to know.

'No. You're the only one.'

'I'm glad. Because I'd hate to compete against any of my friends, really.'

'You'll have to get used to that in show business,' Mr Manyweather told her. 'But this time I think it probably is a good thing.'

'When am I to go?'

'Tomorrow morning. I'll come with you, if you like. I gather your chaperone smashed up the joint last time.'

Maddy giggled reminiscently. 'What shall I wear?' she asked.

'Not black. Not white. Something simple. No frills.'

'My pale blue?' asked Maddy, wishing her mother were near to advise her.

'Blue's a good colour for television. Yes, I should wear that. It's at eleven o'clock. I'll pick you up in front of the Academy at ten-thirty. O.K.?'

'Thank you so much,' beamed Maddy, and hurried back into the classroom, where all her friends started mouthing, 'Have you got it?'

'Camera audition,' she whispered back.

'Quiet, please. We've had enough disturbance this afternoon,' said the geography teacher.

She was a retired headmistress, who came for a few periods a week to instruct the 'Babies'. She did not enjoy the task, for she felt their minds were not really on geography. The occasional absence of pupils to attend auditions worried her considerably. The ballet shoes and fencing foils left lying about in corners seemed out of place to her, and she disliked the constant theatrical gossip that went on.

'It's like a chorus dressing-room, not a classroom,' she would complain.

Next day Maddy was early at the Academy, which seemed strangely quiet in its Saturday morning calm. Only an isolated student rehearsal was going on, and the cleaners were having a good scrub-out, now that there were few students about to trample on the freshly washed floors.

Maddy, tense with determination, stood on the doorstep and waited for Mr Manyweather. She had just *got* to be good.

Eventually 'Agatha' appeared, looking as eccentric as ever.

'Hop in,' shouted Mr Manyweather, who was wearing a strange sort of pirate cap to prevent his hair being blown about. 'We'll have to hurry—we're rather late.'

It was a nightmare journey through the back streets of Kingsway, and Maddy's carefully combed hair was all over the place by the time they arrived. But there was no time to do anything about it. They were due in the studio.

'Aren't I going to have any make-up on?' demanded Maddy, extremely disappointed.

'No, I don't think so. Television make-up is so slight, that they don't bother with children. Schoolgirl complexions are all right without any make-up.'

'From what *I've* seen of most schoolgirls' complexions, they're jolly spotty,' observed Maddy.

They were directed to a small studio, smelling strongly of paint, where there was what appeared to be a drawing-room cut in half, with three cameras trained on it, and the same jumble of cables and lights and microphones that Maddy had seen before. In the middle of it all Morgan Evans stood talking to a girl and two boys.

'Ah, there she is,' he cried, when he saw Maddy, then, 'Leon, my dear fellow. How good of you to come along.'

'I'm doing a spot of chaperoning,' laughed Mr Manyweather.

'Glad to have you here. Will you come up in the gallery with me?'

'No, I think I'm supposed to stay with my charge all the time, aren't I?'

While they talked Maddy looked hard at the other three. With a sinking heart she saw that the girl was much prettier than *she* was. She had brown curly hair and large brown eyes, and lovely teeth. There was something very appealing about her. She was talking and laughing with the two boys with complete unconcern, and yet did not give any impression of showing off. The two boys did not seem to present much competition. One had a funny, humorous face with a turned-up nose and freckles, and the other—the better-looking one— was a bit stolid. But whenever Maddy looked at the girl her own hair felt untidier, her nose felt snubbier, and her dress seemed suddenly to be too short for her.

'Now, I've explained the game to the others,' said Morgan Evans, turning to Maddy. 'And it's really very simple. Are you any good at making up poetry?'

Maddy grimaced.

'Not much.'

'Well, that's all the better, because it makes it funnier. You see, the idea of the game is this. We give you three lines of a verse, and you have to make up a last line. The others on the panel decide if it's good enough to pass. If it's not, you have to pay a forfeit. And here is our chairman, Derek Lacey.'

He indicated a very suave young man, whom Maddy recognised as a minor film star. He was looking rather bored with the whole thing.

'Now, shall we start? Let's make it good—the sponsors are up in the viewing room. I don't mean sponsors—I mean the editorial board of the magazine. If they like this game it'll go into the show.'

'Are they auditioning more than just us four?' Maddy whispered to Mr Manyweather.

'No. They've narrowed it down to you four. So do your best. Don't be afraid to laugh, but don't giggle *too* often. Morgan Evans told me he liked you very much, but was afraid you might be an incorrigible giggler. So just show that you can control it, will you? Don't take any notice of the cameras—you don't need to play to them at all in a panel game.'

Maddy took him at his word and tried to ignore the looming cameras and the suspended mike that swung dangerously over their heads. At first it was difficult, for everything was so strange. They had to sit on quite comfortable chairs in a semicircle, and the question master was at a small desk, with some papers in front of him. They were instructed to smile and say 'Hullo' to one of the cameras when their names were announced. The floor manager stood listening on his headphones to Morgan Evans speaking from the control room. Then he pointed to Derek Lacey, who flashed a toothy smile and started off.

'Hullo, viewers. Today we have a new game for you, called "Poetic Licence". We've four young poets here who are going to show us what they can do, and if they can't do *anything*, then they'll have to pay a forfeit. The idea is that I give each player in turn three lines of a verse, such as

> *Roses are red,*
> *Dandelions are yellow,*
> *And our producer...*

then I stop, and the player has to make up a last line. Now, if he were to add "Is a very fine fellow" he'd be doing very well, wouldn't he? But if he couldn't think of a line, then he'd have to pay a forfeit. Now I'll introduce you to the four would-be poets. First of all, here is Lalage Weinberg. She's fourteen and goes to school in Hendon. Then sitting next to her is Michael Oxley, who's thirteen and at school in Hove.

95

Then Madeleine Fayne, who is fourteen and goes to school right in the heart of London.' Maddy did a rather tremulous grin, and said 'Hullo' much too loudly. 'And finally Philip Manning, also fourteen, who lives in South London and goes to school there. Now, we're all set to start. Have you got your thinking caps on, poets? Remember it'll be much worse if you don't have a shot at a rhyme. Now, here we go.'

Michael Oxley, the freckled boy, couldn't even make an attempt at the first rhyme, and blushed and 'hummed' and 'hawed' for so long that eventually the chairman struck a gong and said, 'I think this calls for a forfeit, don't you?'

'Yes,' agreed the other three, rather timidly.

Michael's forfeit was to pick apples out of a bowl of water, with his mouth. He got so wet and dropped them so often that everyone roared with laughter and the ice was broken.

The verse that the other girl was given was quite easy. It was:

> *'Come into the garden, Maud,*
> *And take a walk with me,*
> *And then we'll go indoors again...'*

'*And have a cup of tea,*' added Lalage, smiling prettily.

'Very good,' praised the chairman. 'Now, Philip, you must help the male side to pull up a bit. Here's yours:

> *'Oh, who will o'er the hills with me*
> *Upon my motor scooter.*
> *It's new and shiny as can be...'*

Philip went hurriedly through the alphabet, murmuring, 'booter, cooter, dooter,' and just as the chairman picked up the stick with which to strike the gong, he shouted, '*But hasn't any hooter.*'

'Jolly good. You nearly got a forfeit, though. Now, Madeleine, here's yours:

> '*Oh where, and oh where*
> *Is my little pussy cat?*
> *She's black and white and furry…*'

Maddy added, '*But not very fat,*' and heaved a sigh of relief to think that the first round was over.

As it became more difficult to find rhymes the answers grew wilder, so that eventually all the players were having to pay forfeits. Maddy quite forgot that it was a camera audition and began to enjoy herself. Even the chairman unbent a little, and dropped his obviously rehearsed attitudes. The worst forfeit Maddy had was to recite 'Sister Susie' while eating a jam puff.

The players were enjoying themselves so much that they were quite surprised when the floor manager made a sign to the chairman, who said, 'Well, that's all for today, I'm afraid. So it's goodbye to you from me, Derek Lacey, and from our four young poets. Say goodbye, all of you.'

The floor manager indicated a camera for them to say goodbye into, and they all chorused goodbyes. Maddy was furious because Lalage blew a kiss towards the camera. She wished Mrs Bosham were there to call her a 'soppy 'aporth'.

They stood about, laughing and talking, until Morgan Evans came down from the gallery. As if by magic the studio had emptied; the bright lights were switched off, and the cameramen, boom-swingers, electricians and engineers had disappeared in an instant.

'Very good,' cried Morgan Evans as he came into the studio. 'Really most amusing. We've made a telerecording, so that we can decide about it at leisure. Now, I'd like you all to come up and meet the sponsors. Oh, dear me, I keep calling them that, but they're not sponsors, they're an editorial board. They're in the viewing room.'

He led the way along seemingly endless corridors to a small, comfortable room with a deep, soft carpet and an enormous television set in one corner, where several rather large gentlemen sat smoking cigars and drinking sherry. Maddy noticed that they were very different from Morgan Evans. They wore proper suits with jackets and trousers that matched, and had stiff collars. There were four of them, and Derek Lacey promptly monopolised the lot, while Maddy, Lalage and the boys stood in a row looking self-conscious. Maddy found the editorial board rather confusing because all wore horn-rimmed spectacles, which made them look alike. At length the four men managed to escape from Derek Lacey, one at a time, and come over to talk to the children. Each asked exactly the same questions, and said that he had enjoyed the programme very much, but no reference was made to any decision about who should get the job.

'And do you read *The World of Youth*?' said one of the editorial board to Maddy.

'No,' replied Maddy.

'Oh, and why not?'

'I don't have time.'

'Don't have time? But what magazine or periodical do you take?'

'None.'

'That's most extraordinary.'

'I can't really afford to,' said Maddy. 'I just read any old magazines that people leave lying around at the Academy.'

'And do they leave *The World of Youth*?'

'No,' said Maddy truthfully. 'It's usually either *The Stage* or *Theatre World*.'

Her questioner sighed and shook his head, and Maddy was certain that she had given the wrong answers.

At last the boys and girls were allowed to leave. Morgan Evans shook hands with each, saying, 'You'll be hearing from us,' and Mr Manyweather, after a hurried conversation with Morgan Evans, said to Maddy, 'Come on, it's lunch-time. I'd better take you back.'

When they were safely ensconced in 'Agatha' and she had been manoeuvred out of the parking place, Maddy said, 'Well?'

'You did very well,' he told her. 'Better than I'd dared to hope. But you're up against pretty strong competition in that other girl. She's very pretty, and she's—well, she's more feminine than you are.'

'I know what you mean,' Maddy agreed glumly. 'I thought she was just a bit soppy, but she's—she's better behaved, somehow.'

'Oh well, we can't really tell. Morgan Evans said he thought you were excellent.'

'But it's those funny old men with spectacles who have the last say, isn't it?' asked Maddy.

'Yes. And they had said they wanted a blond.'

For the rest of the weekend and throughout Monday and Tuesday Maddy turned over and over in her mind her chances of getting the job. On Wednesday afternoon she was hurrying up the stairs of the schoolhouse, late for an English lesson, when a voice behind her called, 'Maddy'.

She turned, and there was Mr Manyweather. He took her by the shoulders saying, 'I was looking for you,' then, gripping her very firmly he said, 'You didn't get it. The other girl did.'

6

LADY LUCK

'Oh,' said Maddy.

It was not until then that she realised how much she had been hoping the job might be hers.

'Cheer up, Maddy,' said Mr Manyweather, seeing the expression on her face. 'You did awfully well. They'll probably remember you for something in the programme—if they use that panel game you may be in it.'

'But the other girl—that Lalage—she'll be in it every week.'

'Yes.'

Maddy nodded miserably. 'I've always been very lucky up till now,' she remarked.

'Beginner's luck,' Mr Manyweather told her. 'Now you're an old stager, and you've got to take the knocks, just like everyone else. But I know how you feel. I'm terribly disappointed too. Look, I've got two free theatre tickets for the Regent Theatre for tonight. I can't go as I have a rehearsal, so would you like to have them?'

'Oh, yes, please,' said Maddy, brightening up. 'And I'll take Zillah. She's never been to a theatre, you know. At least not to a real play, and if she's going to be an actress I think she ought to go. Don't you?'

'I certainly do,' laughed Mr Manyweather—'if she's going to be an actress. And here—here's something to buy ice-cream in the interval.'

And he pressed half a crown into her hand.

'Thanks awfully,' said Maddy, and went into the English class not quite so depressed as she had been a few minutes earlier. She could never keep anything to herself for long, however, and choosing a suitable moment she whispered to Buster:

'I've had it.'

'Had what?'

'That job. I mean I haven't got it.'

'Oh, what a shame.'

Within a few minutes the news had spread round the class and Maddy was receiving sympathetic looks and whispers, but occasionally she caught a gleam of satisfaction in the eyes of those who had gone in for the audition, and had not even got as far as the camera test. Maddy hated to be pitied, so she waved the theatre tickets at Zillah and said, 'We're going on the spree tonight.'

'Where?'

'The *theatre*.'

Zillah's face lit up like a lamp, for one of her biggest ambitions was about to be achieved.

Just then the teacher turned round from the blackboard and said, 'Why is it always Madeleine Fayne who causes disturbances?'

'It's just my nature, I suppose,' said Maddy despairingly, and the class tittered.

'If that was intentional impudence you can go outside.'

'Oh, it wasn't,' said Maddy hastily. 'I'm sorry if it sounded like it.'

'She's had a disappointment,' said Snooks loyally, trying to gloss it over.

'Oh? I'm sorry to hear that, Maddy. But it can't be allowed to interfere with our lesson.'

Maddy reflected that schools must be the same the whole world over. At home in Fenchester she had longed to come to the Academy, and when she heard they were opening a junior department, which included general education as well as dramatic training, she had imagined it would all be quite different from Fenchester High School, and yet she found the teachers said the same sort of things and the pupils made similar replies.

As soon as classes were over Zillah and Maddy hurried back to Fitzherbert Street, changed and bolted their supper. Then, telling Mrs Bosham that they would be late, they set off.

'I can't believe that I be going to the theatre,' said Zillah. In moments of excitement her grammar still went astray, although she had made enormous strides in this first half of the term.

'*Am* going to the theatre,' Maddy corrected her. 'Yes, it's ages since I've been. I can't afford to, on my allowance. I just have to wait for free seats for shows. Still, at the Academy we're quite lucky about comps., though this term there seem to be more for films or television shows than for theatres.'

The play they saw was very light and frothy and amusing and was extremely well acted. Zillah sat enthralled, hardly saying a word, leaning forward in her seat and drinking it all in. During the interval they had ice-creams, although they were the only people in the stalls to do so.

'Well, Mr Manyweather more or less *told* us to,' Maddy excused herself, curling a pink tongue round the inside of her tub, to the disgust of the elderly gentleman sitting next to her.

When the play was over Zillah still seemed in a trance, and it was not until they were out in the street that she spoke.

'Wasn't it wonderful,' she breathed. 'So, that's what we're going to be—actresses like that. I hadn't really understood, you know.'

'You like it better than the cinema then?' asked Maddy curiously.

'Oh, yes; this is—real; it's like the pretence games I used to play,' said Zillah, without realising the contradiction in what she said.

'I know what you mean,' said Maddy. 'It makes everything else seem false. Yes, *I* like the theatre best too. I don't know why I've been so worried about that silly old television.'

The thrill of going to the theatre again, the excitement just before the curtain rose and the satisfaction when it fell, had made her feel that there could not possibly be anything more fascinating. They walked back to Fitzherbert Street exalted and overexcited, Zillah in the first throes of being stage-struck, which Maddy had suffered years earlier. They made wild plans for their futures, that included such decisions as, 'Well, all right, you play leads with the Old Vic, and I'll buy my own theatre in Drury Lane and be actress-manageress.'

When they let themselves in and went down to see Mrs Bosham for the nightly ritual of a cup of cocoa, she said, 'Oh, Maddy, there's bin a phone call fer you, but they wouldn't say who.'

'Funny,' said Maddy. 'Was it a man or a woman?'

'A man—niceish voice. I thought it was one of your brothers at first.'

'Mrs Bosham, I've been telling you for years I haven't *got* a brother.'

'Well, you know who I mean—one of them Blue Door Company—Jeremy or Nigel or that Bulldog—but then they'd've said, knowing it was me.'

'Yes, of course—p'raps it was one of the boys from the Academy about homework or something.'

'Sounded a bit old fer homework,' said Mrs Bosham, who had a nose for a mystery.

Maddy went to bed, still in a happy daze of dreaming about the theatre. She seemed to have been in bed only a very few minutes when the telephone bell pealed again and again through her sleep. Then it stopped, and it was broad daylight and Mrs Bosham was banging on the door, 'Maddy, it's fer you. Merryheather, 'e says 'is name is, though it doesn't seem likely.'

Still half asleep Maddy put on her dressing-gown and stumbled down the stairs. The telephone was an old-fashioned type with separate receiver and speaker, and was fixed to the wall in the hall.

'Hullo,' she said sleepily.

'Hullo, Maddy.'

It was Mr Manyweather's voice. 'Listen, I've got some wonderful news for you. That girl Lalage has appendicitis and so they want you...'

At first it didn't sink in.

'Want me? What for? For the game?'

'No. Wake up. For the whole job. The other girl is ill, and you were second choice. Isn't it wonderful?'

Maddy was suddenly wide awake. 'Gosh, what luck!' she whooped. 'How heavenly—I'm sorry about Lalage, but I'm jolly glad for me. When did you hear?'

'Last night. Morgan Evans rang me in a terrible flap. I knew you were at the theatre, so I couldn't get hold of you at once. He wants you to go round to the office at ten o'clock this morning. You'll have to ring the Academy and get excused your morning lessons. Now, how about a chaperone? I can't manage it today, I'm afraid.'

'Oh dear—well, perhaps Mrs Bosham—must I *really* have one? I know the way to the office all right.'

'No doubt you do, but you *must* have a chaperone—it's the law. We'll have to fix you up with someone, as you'll be doing the whole series.'

'Yes,' said Maddy. 'I don't suppose Mrs Bosham would always be able to spare the time.'

'Mind you, when you're actually working she'd be paid a few guineas for it.'

'Oh, I'll tell her that,' said Maddy, 'but she has got her lodgers to look after, you know. And her cooking to do,' she giggled meaningly.

'Yes, we'll have to go into the subject carefully,' said Mr Manyweather. 'But meanwhile, see if she can go with you just for today; you won't be there long, you know. It's only for you to hear about rehearsal times and so on. Now, behave yourself, won't you?'

'Yes, of course,' said Maddy primly. 'And thank you, Mr Manyweather, because it's all through you...'

'Nonsense; I'm very glad it's come your way after all. Lady Luck certainly smiles on you, Gretchen.'

'Why *Lady* Luck?' demanded Maddy.

'Well, luck *is* a lady. Fickle, you see.' And Mr Manyweather rang off.

Maddy ran up the stairs to where Mrs Bosham was hovering to learn what it was all about.

'I've got it! I've got it after all!' cried Maddy. 'She's ill, and I've got it.'

'What 'ave you got? Is it infectious?' Mrs Bosham demanded in alarm.

'No, no, not the illness—I've got the job! That Lalage girl, the rather soppy, pretty one, has got appendicitis. Isn't it heavenly? I mean, isn't it awful? So I've got the television job.'

'Oh well, I never,' screeched Mrs Bosham in delight, her round face going quite pink with emotion.

'Zillah! Zillah, I've got it after all. Aren't I lucky?' cried Maddy, bouncing into the bedroom.

When the excitement had died down a little Maddy said, 'Mrs Bosham—dear Mrs Bosham—*could* you come with me this morning, just for a little while—to Mr Morgan Evans's office?'

Mrs Bosham frowned. 'There now, dear, I don't think I can manage it. What time does he want you?'

'Ten.'

'Oh, dear me, now. No. I can't; I've got someone coming to look at the first floor front at ten o'clock, so I'm afraid I just can't.'

'Oh dear, whatever shall I do?' wailed Maddy. 'Mr Manyweather says it's the law. I've got to have a grown-up with me all the time. If I let them know it's difficult for me to find one, they might not use me after all. Oh, if only Mummy and Daddy lived in London.' Maddy was nearly in tears of despair. 'If I went to the Academy and explained, they'd send someone with me, a senior or somebody—but there's not time. I've got to be at Kingsway at ten.'

'Wouldn't Zillah do?' asked Mrs Bosham.

'She's not old enough,' objected Maddy. 'She's only a bit older than me.'

'She looks a lot older,' said Mrs Bosham. Maddy began to brighten.

'That's an idea. Zillah, you'd come, wouldn't you?'

'Why, yes,' said Zillah. 'If 'twould be of any use.'

'Good. I think we could make you look old enough,' said Maddy gleefully.

'What on earth do you mean?'

'Mrs Bosham,' wheedled Maddy, 'could we borrow some of your clothes? A hat in particular.'

'Of course,' said Mrs Bosham doubtfully. 'But Zillah'd look a bit funny in my clothes.'

Maddy adored an opportunity to dress anyone up, and fell on the hats in Mrs Bosham's wardrobe with cries of delight. Zillah looked decidedly funny in all of them.

'Don't worry,' said Maddy, 'we'll make you up to match them.'

She got out her stage make-up box, and proceeded to put a heavy character make-up over Zillah's peaches-and-cream complexion. The final effect of Zillah in her own grey coat, with one of Mrs Bosham's more original hats, was startling to say the least.

'No,' said Zillah, putting her foot down at last. 'I won't go out like this. I don't look grown-up. I don't look like anything.' And she wiped off the greasepaint crossly. 'If I come with you, I'll come as myself.'

'But it's no good, unless you look a *bit* older—twenty or so. Here, put your hair up on top.'

They pinned her hair up on the top of her head, then Maddy took the flowers and a piece of veiling off one of Mrs Bosham hats and made a tiny little frothy hat to perch on top.

'There, now—just a touch of make-up. Put it on yourself if you don't trust me—and have those earrings of Mrs Bosham's.'

When she was finished Zillah looked a trifle odd, but had certainly added a few years to her appearance.

'I wish you'd got some high heels,' said Maddy, looking at her appraisingly. 'Still, you're quite tall beside me.'

Zillah did not possess any stockings, so with an eyebrow pencil Maddy drew seams down the back of her legs very effectively.

'Come on,' said Maddy, 'we must fly now.'

'Good luck!' Mrs Bosham called after them. 'Don't worry. Zillah looks a proper grown-up young lady!'

But nevertheless there was something just a little strange about Zillah's appearance, for people turned to stare as the girls hurried, almost running, through back streets and short-cuts to the enormous building in Kingsway.

Maddy was so excited that she was panting and giggling at the same time, and they had to stand still to collect themselves before they went in.

Morgan Evans's office had been changed again, but the new one was larger, and was just as full and as busy as ever. Telephones were ringing, people dashing in and out, the typewriter adding its clickety-clack to the clamour.

'I'm so glad that you could step into the breach,' Morgan Evans said, smiling kindly at Maddy, then casting a doubtful glance at Zillah.

'Er—this is Miss Pendray, my chaperone,' said Maddy, stifling a giggle. 'She—she doesn't speak English very well.'

'Oh well, do take a seat, mademoiselle,' said Morgan Evans, speaking loudly and clearly.

Zillah turned scarlet as she sat down, and wondered why she had ever allowed Maddy to get her into such a ridiculous situation.

'I just want to make sure you know what you're letting yourself in for,' said Morgan Evans to Maddy. 'This programme is contracted for fourteen weeks, and it'll mean you're working all day every Saturday for nearly four months. You'll also have to rehearse half-days during the week. Now, when do you have your school lessons, and when do you have acting lessons?'

'Acting in the mornings and lessons in the afternoons,' said Maddy.

'That's awkward of you,' said Morgan Evans, making a wry face. 'Lalage was the other way round—so we've said rehearsals in the afternoons. Still, they can be changed. You do realise, don't you, that yours will be a most important part of the show. It will be a sort of magazine programme with different items each week, but *you* will be going all the way through. It's going to mean a great deal of work for you. Now, all the business of a contract has to be settled, and that will have to be fixed between your parents and our contracts department. Will you please give your father's address and phone number to my secretary.'

While Maddy was doing this Morgan Evans turned to Zillah and said brightly, '*Parlez-vous français, mademoiselle?*'

Zillah just looked at him blankly, because she didn't.

'No,' said Maddy hastily. 'She doesn't. It makes it very difficult.'

Morgan Evans seemed surprised, and kept glancing at Zillah in a doubtful manner.

'The first rehearsal will be next Monday,' Morgan Evans told Maddy. 'Now, I'd better ring your school and make quite sure that it's all right with them.'

'Oh, it will be,' said Maddy. 'After all, it was entirely through Mr Manyweather...'

'Next thing—rehearsals. These will be held in the St Adelaide's Youth Club in Russell Square.'

'Not here?' put in Maddy, rather disappointed.

'Oh, no, no. We shan't get into the studio until the Saturday of each week, unfortunately. Not enough studio space, you see.'

'Oh, I see,' said Maddy, though she didn't really.

'Now, about clothes,' said Morgan Evans. 'What is your wardrobe like? You've looked very nice each time I've seen you, and quite suitably turned out for the programme. But is what I've seen the full extent of your wardrobe, or have you plenty of clothes?'

'No, I haven't,' said Maddy bluntly. 'You've seen the only decent things I've got. I keep them for special occasions. Most of the time I wear shabby old slacks and jeans, don't I, Zill—er—Miss Pendray?'

Zillah looked terrified and Maddy said hastily, 'Oh, I forgot—it's no good talking to her.'

'Well, I suggest that you wear your own clothes, at any rate for the first few weeks, then if necessary we shall replace them from our wardrobe, which means that our wardrobe people will make or buy them for you, but they'll be your own to keep, you see. Any fancy sort of clothes you may need will be hired, of course. All right?'

'Lovely,' said Maddy. 'I'm longing to know what I've actually got to *do*.'

'You'll hear all about that on Monday,' said Morgan Evans. 'We're hoping to get out some sort of script before then, and we'll send you a copy. Oh, by the way, on Monday there'll be some press photographers at the rehearsal, so don't wear your "shabby old slacks and jeans", will you? Try to have on the rig-out you'll wear for the first programme. We're having two weeks' rehearsal for the first one, just to make sure, with a "dry run" on Saturday week.'

'What in the world's a "dry run"?' asked Maddy.

'It's really what your audition was,' said Morgan Evans. 'The performance is put on exactly as though it is a real show, with cameras and everything, but it is not transmitted.'

'Oh, good,' said Maddy. 'I'm glad I'll have a nice lot of practice first.'

'Well, I think that's about all,' said Morgan Evans, and two telephones rang at once, so Maddy and Zillah stood awkwardly, waiting till he had finished on the telephones so that they could say goodbye.

Just as they were going out of the door Morgan Evans called Maddy back again.

'Maddy,' he said, 'are you quite sure your chaperone is over twenty-one?'

'Er—no—she's not quite,' said Maddy.

'I thought not. And you really ought to have someone who can speak English, you know.'

Maddy gulped back a giggle. 'She may learn—quite quickly.'

'Yes, but it's got to be someone over twenty-one. Tell them at your school they must make some other arrangements. We shall pay a fee of a few guineas, you know.'

'Yes, I'll tell them,' said Maddy, and escaped hurriedly to Zillah, who was almost in tears of embarrassment in the corridor.

'Oh, Maddy, you shouldn't have,' she gasped. 'I felt so awful—and they might have been cross—and you might have lost the job.'

'Don't be silly. It was perfectly all right,' said Maddy, 'and it got me out of a hole. Thanks awfully, Zillah.'

'Well, I'm never going to do it again,' said Zillah.

'You're ungrateful, then,' said Maddy crossly. 'I took you out of that beastly hostel, and—and took you to Mrs Bosham's, and took you to the theatre, and—and you grumble over doing a little thing like this for me.'

Zillah sighed. She was finding that it was impossible to argue with Maddy.

Back in the office Morgan Evans was saying, 'What an extraordinary chaperone.'

'Most odd,' agreed his secretary.

'I somehow feel,' said Morgan Evans, 'that there isn't going to be a dull moment on this show with Miss Fayne about.'

7

SUNNY

The next day a large envelope addressed to Maddy arrived at 37 Fitzherbert Street. Inside was a television script, duplicated on many pages of peculiar buff-coloured paper, and Maddy was horrified to see how much she had to say.

The magazine with which the programme was connected, *The World of Youth*, was intended for twelve-year-olds and upwards. It had an accent on friendship with children of other countries, and encouraged pen pals to write to each other all over the world. Every week the programme was to include a playlet set in a different country, in which Maddy was to play the part of an English girl on a trip round the world, and where each week girls and boys from foreign countries who were visiting England would come to the studios and Maddy would interview them. There was to be a certain amount of singing and dancing in which Maddy would not be taking part.

'Thank goodness I'm not,' said Maddy. 'I've got absolutely oceans to learn—I'll never do it.'

'I'll hear your lines,' volunteered Zillah.

'Thanks. Oh, isn't it exciting—but isn't it terrifying?'

In the afternoon Maddy had an appointment to see Mrs Seymore about the television series. When a message came for her in the middle of French dictation she hurried round to the Academy, only too pleased to escape, and knocked on Mrs Seymore's door.

'Come in, Maddy, and sit down,' said Roma Seymore kindly. 'I'm just having a cup of tea. Will you have one?'

'Yes, please,' said Maddy promptly, eyeing the plate of buns.

'And take a bun too. Now, my dear, we've a lot of things to think about, haven't we?'

'Gosh, yes,' said Maddy. 'I should just think so.'

'And please don't say "Gosh" on television, will you?' Maddy looked guilty.

'I'll try not to.'

'Now, you fully understand, don't you, that being on this programme must *not* be allowed to interfere with your schoolwork?'

'Oh, yes, Mrs Seymore.'

'Well, had the whole series been during the term I don't know that it would have been wise to undertake it at all, but by the time the series is well under way it will be the summer vacation, when you will have plenty of time. I understand you've spoken to your parents about it.'

'Yes, I rang them last night. They're very pleased.'

'So I believe. I rang them this morning, and we had quite a long talk. Now, next we must set about getting you a licence to act. As you've had one before that should not be difficult, but what does worry me is the question of a chaperone. Morgan Evans rang me this morning and asked if I could find a more suitable one. Afterwards I wondered what he meant by "more suitable". More suitable than whom?'

Maddy blushed.

'Oh, just a girl who went with me to his office yesterday. He didn't think she looked old enough.'

'I see. Well. We'll have to do something about it quickly. What we need is a nice respectable woman between thirty and forty, who wants to earn a little pin-money. I think I'll put an advertisement in the evening paper tomorrow. We really need someone by Monday, don't we? This business of chaperones is rather a problem. Several of the acting schools that are also agencies have their own chaperones, but as we have so few pupils under fifteen at the Academy we've never found it necessary.'

'If only my mother were here...'

'Yes, I know, dear. It is difficult for you. But we must keep to the rules of the London County Council, otherwise there might be trouble about you doing the work at all. Yes, I think I'll put the advertisement in tomorrow, and give my home phone number, then interview applicants on Sunday.'

'Thank you, Mrs Seymore,' said Maddy gratefully. 'I'm sorry you've got to take all this trouble.'

'And will you come round on Sunday afternoon and meet the chaperone? After all, it would be awkward if I engaged someone and you disliked each other at first sight. If there are several applicants I'll narrow them down to two or three.'

'I'd love to come,' said Maddy. 'What time?'

'About four. And I'll provide something a little more filling than Academy buns.'

Mrs Seymore's fine eyes twinkled as she noted the empty plate.

'Oh, sorry,' said Maddy guiltily. 'French *dictée* always makes me hungry.'

'Well, you'd better hurry back before the lesson's completely over,' smiled Mrs Seymore. 'You know where my flat is, don't you?'

'Yes,' said Maddy. 'You had us there for the carol rehearsals.'

'So I did. Well, four o'clock then, on Sunday.'

Maddy worked on her script throughout Saturday, and found that it was not too difficult to learn after all, as it was in a very easy conversational style.

'I don't expect I'll have to keep exactly to the script later on,' she said to Zillah. 'But for this first one I'd better, just to make sure.'

On Sunday morning they went to St Martin-in-the-Fields, then Maddy did some more study, and at a quarter to four she set off for Mrs Seymore's flat. It was within easy walking distance, and she reached it promptly at four. It was a first-floor flat in a tall house in a quiet square, and had large spacious rooms—somewhat austerely but tastefully furnished—that came as a pleasant relief after 'The Boshery', as Maddy sometimes called 37 Fitzherbert Street.

'I've narrowed them down to two,' Roma Seymore greeted her, 'a Miss Chittock and a Miss Mackenzie should be here at any minute.'

Just then the bell rang.

Mrs Seymore went to answer the door, and Maddy looked round the room hopefully. She could see the tea things, but no food—and Mrs Seymore had promised something solid.

Mrs Seymore reappeared shortly, talking over her shoulder to someone. She was rather pink in the face and not nearly as composed as usual.

'This is the girl for whom we are wanting a chaperone,' she was saying as she came in. And then Miss Mackenzie entered, and Maddy's eyes nearly popped out of her head. For Miss Mackenzie was a black lady.

She was a tall woman, broad and plump, wearing a red patterned dress and a blue hat, but the most noticeable thing about her was her smile. It was wide and warm, and her large black eyes sparkled with good humour.

'Good afternoon,' said Maddy in a rather subdued voice.

'Why, hullo, honey—I thought it was going to be a grown-up young lady wanting a chaperone,' she said, with a slight American accent.

'No, you see, it's like this,' Mrs Seymore began, offering Miss Mackenzie a chair, and proceeding to explain the situation. When she had finished Miss Mackenzie asked candidly:

'And you would not mind having a lady of colour to look after her?'

Maddy and Mrs Seymore glanced at each other and then back to Miss Mackenzie.

'Of course we wouldn't mind,' said Maddy promptly, for she had taken to Miss Mackenzie on sight.

'Well, we'd never really considered...' began Mrs Seymore. 'It's a little unusual in England, but...'

'I know, I know. I came here with an American family five years ago, looking after the kids. Now my young 'uns they've growed up and go to school, but this family they're so kind to me they say, "You stay here, live with us still, but find some little job during the daytime to keep you busy." So I says to myself, "Sunny"—that's my name—"Sunny, this is just the job for you."'

'H'm.' Mrs Seymore looked at her speculatively. She seemed eminently suitable, but just a little startling.

''Course—my lady, she'll give me some lovely references.'

'I'm sure of that,' said Mrs Seymore. 'Now do have a cup of tea. I have a few more applications to see.'

Maddy was longing to say, 'Please let's have this one.' But knew that it would be tactless, so contented herself with beaming at Miss Mackenzie and plying her with the cakes which Mrs Seymore had produced from the sideboard.

'I sure would like to do this job for you, ma'am,' said Miss Mackenzie earnestly, biting into a bun. 'This T.V.—it sounds great—I'd sure like to...'

'How many children are you used to looking after?'

'Three—two boys and a girl.'

'Then I think you could just about cope with Maddy,' smiled Mrs Seymore.

Miss Mackenzie laughed heartily and turned to Maddy. 'So you're going to be an actress?' she said. 'My, my. And you just a scrap of a girl—I'd a thought you was too young...'

'Oh, no,' said Maddy. 'You see, I shall still have to do my school lessons during term. But there aren't many more weeks of term. Then in the holidays I'll be able to do as much rehearsing for television as they want.'

'Yes, after the end of term she would probably be needing someone all day, instead of for mornings only, and all day Saturdays,' explained Mrs Seymore. 'That would be all right with you?'

'Fine, just fine.'

Miss Mackenzie got up to go.

'Well, I hope you decide to take me ma'am. You call my lady. Here's the phone number. She'll tell you I'm the honest-est, God-fearingest gal. And I know we'd be mighty happy.'

'Goodbye, Miss Mackenzie,' said Maddy. 'I *do* hope I'll see you again.'

Miss Mackenzie gave Maddy an enormous wink while Mrs Seymore wasn't looking, and sailed out of the room.

Mrs Seymore saw her to the door, then came back into the room and flopped on to the sofa, laughing.

'Well, what a surprise! When I opened the door you could have knocked me down with the proverbial feather!'

'But isn't she heavenly?' cried Maddy. 'I do like her. Can't I have her Mrs Seymore?'

'Well, I don't know.' Mrs Seymore seemed quite at a loss. 'I liked her too. She's a real character. But I'm afraid she'd cause rather a stir. You really should have someone—less noticeable.'

'But people would get used to her,' Maddy argued desper-ately. 'It's only because of her colour, isn't it?'

'Yes, Maddy. But people can be so unkind. And you're going to have enough to worry about without having to wonder if your chaperone is meeting with approval,' said Mrs Seymore sensibly.

'Yes, I see what you mean. But I feel sure she can look after herself.'

'Um—but the point is, she's supposed to look after *you*. However, we'll see what the other one is like before deciding. What's her name? Miss Chittock.'

'I don't like the sound of it,' said Maddy. 'I like Miss Mackenzie's name—Sunny. It suits her—it's like her smile.'

Just then the bell rang, and Mrs Seymore hurried off to answer it. When she returned with Miss Chittock, Maddy's heart sank. Miss Chittock was small and dried up, and wore a grey coat and a very unbecoming brown hat. She had no make-up on, and wore a sour expression as though she had just sucked a lemon.

'And this is the child?' she demanded, looking at Maddy up and down disapprovingly. Maddy looked back equally disapprovingly.

'Yes, this is Madeleine,' said Mrs Seymore in a forcedly cheerful voice. 'And as I explained to you on the phone, it would mean chaperoning her to the television studios, and anywhere else she might have to go.'

'H'm, I've never done any of this chaperoning business. I've been a governess for twenty years. There wouldn't be any lessons to give?'

'No, I'm afraid not,' Mrs Seymore said firmly. 'Maddy receives her education at the British Actors' Guild Junior Academy. She has acting lessons for half the day and school lessons for the other half.'

'School lessons for only half the day? I shouldn't have thought that would be sufficient.'

Miss Chittock's long nose quivered disapprovingly.

'Our examination results are excellent,' said Mrs Seymore sweetly, 'so it would seem to be adequate. Do have a cup of tea.'

Maddy looked closely at Mrs Seymore. She suspected that they both disliked Miss Chittock, but Mrs Seymore was being so charming that it was difficult to tell.

'Of course, I don't know that I approve of a child *acting* on *television*.'

'Good,' thought Maddy. 'That settles it—Mrs Seymore will never have her now.'

'Oh, that's a pity,' said Mrs Seymore in a rather brittle voice. 'Then you wouldn't consider the post, I take it. Oh well...'

'No, no, I don't say that,' replied Miss Chittock hastily. 'It's just that it seems—well—a little unusual.'

'It is,' agreed Mrs Seymore. 'You see, Maddy's parents don't live in London, otherwise her mother would be able to chaperone her. What we really want is to find a nice dependable person to take the place of her mother.'

'Well. I'm sure I'm dependable enough.' Miss Chittock bristled, as though her honesty had been questioned. 'I worked for ten years in the same situation until my charge went to finishing school. My references are impeccable.' She made a sort of pecking movement as she said 'impeccable' that almost made Maddy laugh.

'Oh, I'm quite sure they are, but—er—do you think you would be quite happy in the atmosphere of—er—the entertainment world?' asked Mrs Seymore.

'I've always managed to interest myself in whatever strata of society I have found myself,' said Miss Chittock, pursing her lips into a self-righteous expression.

After that the conversation flagged. Miss Chittock refused a cake, but just sat there, making no effort to go. At last

Mrs Seymore said with an air of finality, 'Well, thank you very much for coming along, Miss Chittock. I have some more applicants to interview, but if you will leave me your address and phone number...'

Miss Chittock wrote it down, in a rather spidery handwriting, that Maddy thought looked exactly like her. Even then she did not seem anxious to go, and began talking about 'Young people these days', and airing her pet theories on education. Maddy kept very quiet, for she knew that if she spoke she would say something impolite, and Mrs Seymore would not like it.

At last Miss Chittock gathered up her drab handbag, pulled on her meticulously darned grey cotton gloves, shook hands with Maddy in a bony grip and was gone. When Mrs Seymore returned from seeing her out, looking rather worried, Maddy said, 'Are those the only two who are coming?'

'Yes, Maddy, I'm afraid so. I didn't weed them out very well, did I? But all the others either asked too high a fee, or else could only manage the weekday mornings, not Saturdays. It's really most difficult. And you simply must have someone by tomorrow.'

'*Couldn't* I have that nice Sunny Mackenzie?' begged Maddy. 'I did think she was so nice.'

'Certainly, compared to Miss Chittock...' Mrs Seymore left the sentence unfinished. She thought for a few minutes and then said, 'Well, Maddy, let's ask Miss Mackenzie to do it for a trial week. Of course, Morgan Evans may not like the idea.'

'*He* wouldn't object to Sunny,' said Maddy. 'As long as she is over twenty-one he wouldn't care if she was tartan. Shall we ring her up now and tell her?'

'Don't rush me, Maddy,' smiled Mrs Seymore. 'She may not have had time to get home yet. Oh well, I could ring her employer, and ask for a reference.'

'Yes, that's a good idea,' said Maddy eagerly.

Mrs Seymore dialled the number, and a high-pitched American voice answered. To all Mrs Seymore's questions there came a flow of praise for Miss Mackenzie that was absolutely overwhelming. When Mrs Seymore put down the phone she appeared to be entirely satisfied.

'Well, that seems quite all right. Sunny has been with them for several years, and they have found her to be just as nice as we felt she was. Her employer says they consider her almost one of the family, and can't bear the thought of losing her, even though the children she used to look after now go to school.'

'Oh, how heavenly,' cried Maddy, clapping her hands. 'I just couldn't have had that terrible Miss Chittock.'

'I'll ring Miss Mackenzie as soon as she's had time to get in, and tell her to meet you—where? Outside the Academy tomorrow morning. You know where the rehearsal is to be, don't you?'

'Yes, in Russell Square,' said Maddy. 'I'll show her the way. Don't you worry, Mrs Seymore, I'll look after her all right.'

Mrs Seymore laughed.

'That is not really supposed to be the idea, Maddy. As I've told you, the chaperone is supposed to look after you—that's why I'm a trifle worried. After all, she is a foreigner and mayn't know all our ways.'

'Don't worry,' Maddy repeated. 'I'm sure it'll be O.K. And she's been in England a long time, hasn't she?'

'Oh, yes, yes.'

'And we couldn't have had Miss Chittock. Why, she didn't even approve of acting. She'd have *hated* the television studios.'

'Yes, you're right, Maddy. I just wonder whether we ought to advertise again.'

'Well, let's wait and see how dear Sunny gets on,' urged Maddy. 'Isn't it a suitable name?'

'Yes, Maddy, but you must call her Miss Mackenzie, unless she asks you to use her Christian name.'

'Yes, Mrs Seymore,' said Maddy meekly, although her eyes were beaming with delight at having got her own way. 'I think I'd better go now and study some more of my part. Thank you ever so much for giving up your Sunday afternoon on my account.'

'It's been very interesting,' laughed Mrs Seymore. 'Well, I hope you get on all right tomorrow morning. Whatever happens, don't be late for school in the afternoon, because if the television work appears to interfere with your schooling Mr Whitfield won't let you do it at all, you know.'

Maddy could not really imagine Mr Whitfield behaving so cruelly, but she said meekly, 'No, I won't be late. They've arranged the rehearsals to fit in with school hours, so I should think they're sure to let me off in time.'

'Well, good luck, Maddy. I know you won't let us down. Don't forget to take a nice sharp pencil with you tomorrow and mark down on your script your moves and things that the producer tells you.'

'No, I won't forget. Though it's funny how pencils *will* break just before a first rehearsal.'

'Yes, I've noticed that too,' laughed Mrs Seymore, as she walked down the stairs with Maddy. 'Well, take more than one and be on the safe side.'

Maddy said goodbye with renewed thanks, and added, 'When you ring Sun—er—I mean Miss Mackenzie—tell her I'm very glad it's her, won't you?'

'Yes,' said Mrs Seymore. 'I will.'

Maddy went happily back to Fitzherbert Street, and entertained Zillah and Mrs Bosham with imitations of the two applicants for the post of chaperone.

'Sunny's a lady of colour,' explained Maddy. 'That's what she called herself, and that's what she is. You'll simply love her.'

All that evening Maddy studied her lines, with Zillah hearing her and prompting gently in her soft low voice, which was gradually losing its country burr.

When she went to bed Maddy was so excited that she could not sleep. She kept thinking how awful it would have been if she had had Miss Chittock instead of Miss Sunny Mackenzie—and then she would start wondering about the next day's rehearsal. She was extremely grateful to have had some training with Mr Manyweather, as without it she would have felt at a complete loss.

Next morning she awoke early for fear of oversleeping, and was soon wandering round the room getting her things ready.

'I'm sorry I can't go in my slacks, but Morgan Evans said the press photographers will be there,' she told Zillah. 'I must wear the dress I'll have on for the actual programme. That'll be my pale blue. Oh dear, I've got to press it, and I simply *must* do something about hair ribbons—or do you think slides will be all right?'

'Oh, don't fuss so,' murmured Zillah sleepily. 'Don't fuss.'

'It's all very well for you,' snapped Maddy. 'This isn't the most important day of your life, but for me it is—or very nearly.'

Throughout breakfast she repeatedly urged Zillah not to be late if she wanted to walk to the Academy with her, but finally it was Zillah who was kept waiting, for at the last minute Maddy couldn't find her script.

'I do hope Sunny will be there,' Maddy kept saying as they set off. Sure enough as they rounded the corner there was Miss Mackenzie's tall, broad figure planted firmly outside the Academy. She wore a royal-blue dress of rather strange cut, and a red hat with a large pigeon perched on top of it. 'Evidently red and blue are her favourite colours,' thought Maddy.

Zillah almost stood still in amazement. 'So *that's* her, Maddy!' she breathed.

'Yes,' chuckled Maddy. 'There's no chance of missing her, is there?'

'Hullo there, honey,' Sunny greeted her. 'I sure am glad to be seeing you today. I was half afeared that nice lady of yours might have chosen someone else.'

'And I'm glad to see you too,' said Maddy. 'This is my friend Zillah. She goes to the Academy, but she's not coming to the television rehearsal. Not today, anyhow. But I'm going to try and work her in at the very first opportunity. Come on, though, we'll have to get a move on. Bye, Zillah. See you this afternoon and tell you all about it.'

They walked through to Russell Square: Sunny with her long loose strides and Maddy hurrying along beside her, giving a hop, skip and a jump every now and then in order to keep up.

'That person who came after you was *awful*!' Maddy told her. 'She looked like a—a vinegar bottle. And she didn't approve of television, and she didn't approve of children acting, and I'm sure she wouldn't have approved of me.'

'I know,' giggled Sunny. 'I waited outside to see what she done look like, and when I seen her I says to myself, "I sure do hope that Miss Madeleine don't have to stomach that old sour-puss."'

Maddy laughed delightedly.

'I say, Sunny, *please* don't call me Miss Madeleine. Call me Maddy, like everyone else does, and I'll call you Sunny—if you don't mind, that is.'

Sunny frowned. 'Well, I don't know, Miss Maddy. It don't seem quite proper somehow.'

'Don't be silly,' said Maddy. 'Didn't you call the children you were looking after just by their Christian names?'

'No, miss. Not after they were babies. They were Master Elmer, Master Glyn and Miss Kate as soon as they were knee high to a grasshopper, as you might say.'

'Oh well, it's quite different in television,' said Maddy sweepingly. 'Everybody calls everybody by their Christian names, so you'll have to, too.'

'Just like you say, Miss Maddy, honey,' said Sunny doubtfully. 'I'll try to remember in front of other folks, but when we're alone I guess you'll just have to put up with being Miss Maddy.'

Maddy laughed. 'You are funny,' she cried. 'You'll be the best chaperone anyone ever had, I'm sure.'

'I don't know nothing about television,' said Sunny. 'Is it very difficult? What will I have to do? Mrs Seymore didn't explain very much.'

'Well, yes, television is difficult,' said Maddy. 'But you won't really have a lot to do, except see that I'm all right. And I'm pretty nearly always all right. But you have to go everywhere I go—into the studio, to meals, in the dressing-room, even to have a wash.'

'What—even go to the bathroom with you?' demanded Sunny in horror.

'Yes,' laughed Maddy. 'Isn't it ridiculous? Anyone would think I was still a child.'

This time it was Sunny's turn to laugh. She threw back her head.

'You're a caution, honey,' she cried, and Maddy joined in her laughter.

There was a peculiarly comforting quality about Sunny that Maddy had never met before. From feeling nervous and a little unsure of herself because it was to be a first rehearsal in a new medium, she began to feel confident and happy. It was so strange and new to have an attendant like Sunny, who adopted the role of servant yet without becoming servile. Maddy remembered some of her mother's charwomen and maids, who had been determined not to be put upon in any way, and she could not help contrasting their attitude with Sunny's pleasing manner.

Just then they came in sight of a long low wooden build-ing, standing on a bombed site.

'This is the rehearsal room,' said Maddy. And they turned in at the door.

8

MISS TIBBS

Maddy did not quite know what she had expected to find on entering the building, but it was certainly not the scene that met their eyes when they stepped over the threshold. The amazing thing was that it looked just like a room at the Academy, set out for one of Mr Manyweather's television rehearsals. It was almost completely bare, except for some upright wooden chairs arranged in strange patterns on the floor, following a design mapped out in chalks of various colours. In one corner a group of people stood talking and laughing, but they all stopped and turned towards the door when they heard it open.

'Ah, good, it's Madeleine,' said Morgan Evans, advancing towards her. Then he saw Sunny, and stopped dead.

'Er—yes, madam, can I help you?' he asked politely.

'Oh, it's all right, she's with me,' said Maddy. 'I must introduce you. Mr Evans, this is my chaperone, Miss Mackenzie—and she's over twenty-one.'

Mr Morgan Evans quickly came over his astonishment.

'Oh well, that's a good thing. I—er—I'm glad you could come, Miss Mackenzie. Now come along, Maddy, and meet everyone.'

Maddy recognised one of the elderly men, who was beautifully dressed and most important-looking, as a member of the editorial board she had seen at the camera audition.

'This is Mr Stanley,' said Morgan Evans, 'the editor of *The World of Youth*. He wants to say a few words before we start the rehearsal.'

Mr Stanley was staring fixedly at Sunny, who grinned broadly back at him.

'Oh, yes—yes,' he said hurriedly and turned to survey the company.

'Before you start work I just wanted to say to you that although *The World of Youth* is a commercial concern and has to pay its way just like any other publication, its proprietors have imbued it with a very high sense of purpose—that of friendship between the nations. And we know that it is with the young people of the world that our hope lies. Therefore, although we want this show to be lively, slick and full of fun, we also want from each and every one of you a feeling of sincerity and purpose.'

He had obviously learned his speech by heart, but somehow the presence of Sunny seemed to put him off. His eyes kept straying back to her and he would 'um' and 'ah' uncertainly. When he had finished saying the same thing several times, but couched in different words, everyone nodded sagely and said, 'M'm' or 'Yes' very sincerely, but Sunny said loudly, 'Too true, Mr Stanley, sir, too true.'

Then Mr Stanley turned to Morgan Evans in puzzlement.

'Morgan,' he asked, 'is this lady in the show?'

'No, no,' said Morgan Evans hastily. 'She's Madeleine's chaperone, Miss Mackenzie.'

'Well, she *should* take part in the show,' said Mr Stanley. 'Write her in. Goodbye, everyone.'

And he left the hall abruptly. Morgan Evans flopped into a chair while there was a buzz of excitement from the rest of the cast.

'Write her in,' moaned Morgan Evans. 'Just like that. Oh, preserve us.' He said something in Welsh that did not sound at all polite.

Maddy and Sunny looked at each other in a worried fashion, as they could not quite understand what was going on.

'Miss Tibbs,' cried Morgan Evans, 'where are you?'

Maddy now noticed an elderly woman, with cropped grey hair, who hurried forward to the producer saying, 'Don't worry—don't worry—it's the perfect answer. We wondered what we ought to do about the child's parents—why they never appear in the script. This is the perfect answer—she's attended by the faithful family retainer—our friend here.'

'It's an idea,' said Morgan Evans slowly, appearing to recover a little. 'But can she act?'

Miss Tibbs turned to Sunny. 'Can you act?' she demanded sternly, seeming to dare her to say no.

'Well, ma'am, I ain't never tried,' said Sunny equably.

All the rest of the cast roared with laughter, and Sunny grinned in a friendly fashion, not taking the least offence.

Morgan Evans looked at Sunny speculatively.

'H'm, well, she's got a good sense of timing,' he observed, then suddenly he seemed to brighten. 'Yes, it's an excellent idea,' he said. 'It'll make the show. You write her just a few lines, Miss Tibbs, but make them *good*. Can you do it by tomorrow?'

'Trust me,' said Miss Tibbs stoutly, nodding her head in determination.

Nobody had actually asked Sunny whether she'd like to be in the show, and Maddy thought it was time they did.

'Would you like it, Sunny?' she asked. 'Like to be actually in the show instead of just watching?'

'Suits me fine, Miss Maddy,' said Sunny happily. 'Just whatever the folks want.'

'Of course, she'll be paid more than for chaperoning, won't she, Mr Evans?' said Maddy.

'Oh, yes, of course you will, my dear Miss—er—Mackenzie, of course. And now we must have a read-through of the script, even though it will have to be amended by tomorrow.'

At one end of the room some of the wooden-backed chairs had been drawn round a table and Morgan Evans settled himself between his secretary and Miss Tibbs. The cast arranged themselves on the chairs and the read-through began.

'Try to bash straight through,' said Morgan Evans. 'We want to get a rough idea of the timing, and in the interview I wonder if perhaps—er—Miss Mackenzie, would you mind answering the questions that Maddy asks you? We're not quite sure yet what nationality we're going to have for the dry run.'

This didn't mean a thing to Sunny, but she nodded happily.

'Now, we start off with the interview after Maddy's opening remarks. All set, everyone?'

He looked questioningly at his secretary, who was holding a stopwatch poised.

'Right,' she said, and clicked a knob.

'Off you go then.'

Maddy had studied her script so well that she knew it nearly by heart, therefore she could read it perfectly, and she delivered her opening lines with great aplomb, but when it came to the interview Sunny's replies were so quaint that she and everyone else was convulsed with laughter.

The questions that Maddy had to ask were framed to suit a schoolchild, and when Maddy asked, 'And tell me, what sort of school do you go to in America?' Sunny answered, 'I reckon I'm too big a girl for school, Miss Maddy.'

Morgan Evans, with tears of laughter rolling down his face, kept urging them to keep on, and not to stop or the timing would be lost. When Maddy finished up with, 'Well, thank you for coming to visit us on our programme today, and *bon voyage*,' Sunny retaliated with, 'I guess you ain't getting rid of me easy as that, Miss Maddy.'

Exhausted with laughter, Morgan Evans said, 'Right, give us the announcement for the musical part of the show, Maddy, then we can hold it.'

The next part of the show included a troupe of dancers from Spain and a French boy pianist who was in London to give a concert at the Albert Hall.

'But we shan't have them here until the day of the programme,' explained Morgan Evans. 'That interview was one of the funniest things I've heard for a long time,' he went on.

'Miss Tibbs, see you give Miss Mackenzie some good comedy lines in the sketch.'

Miss Tibbs was scribbling away rapidly in a notebook.

'Rather,' she agreed. 'She's given me some ideas already.'

'Now,' said Morgan Evans, 'we come to the sketch, which affects everyone. The idea is that Maddy, an English school-girl, is on a trip round the world, and each week she visits a different country. The first sketch, for the dry run, and the next few, will be done in the studio, but eventually—well, we have some rather different plans.'

The first sketch was about South America, and Maddy now noticed that all the actors were dark-skinned and swarthy. Although they were English, several of them could speak Spanish, and had to do so for a few lines of the script. A girl of about seventeen or eighteen was playing the part of an Argentinian schoolgirl.

'I've got it!' cried Miss Tibbs suddenly, waving her notebook.

'Yes, yes? What?' demanded Morgan Evans.

'Instead of having the child, Madeleine, just floating round the world for no apparent reason, why don't we have her coming back from—oh—somewhere, where her parents are living—on her way to boarding school in England, and just stopping off at various countries on the way. What do you think?'

'It's an idea,' said Morgan Evans, 'and it accounts for Miss Mackenzie nicely too. We'll have to see what Mr Stanley thinks about it. But what country?'

'Mr Stanley will have to decide that,' said Miss Tibbs firmly. 'But I do think it is an angle.'

Everybody listened interestedly.

'Yes,' said Rita, the seventeen-year-old girl. 'I have thought it's a trifle odd at present, the way the English child just sort of appears in the sketch—there should be some reason for her wandering round the world.'

'P'raps I've got a magic carpet,' said Maddy hopefully.

'We toyed with that idea,' said Miss Tibbs, 'but came to the conclusion that *The World of Youth* is more down-to-earth and factual than that. No, I think we've hit it now. And I'll rewrite the first transmission script to include some lines of dialogue between Madeleine and Miss Mackenzie to explain the whole situation.'

'Now then, let's read the sketch through as it stands,' said Morgan Evans. 'But don't forget, it'll be altered tomorrow.'

Everybody laughed good-naturedly.

They all read extremely well, and Maddy felt quite nervous because their standard was so high. The sketch was interesting, but completely without humour, and when they had finished reading they discovered it had taken a few minutes under the quarter of an hour it was supposed to last.

'That's all to the good, Miss Tibbs. It will be easier for you to write in Miss Mackenzie's part. You won't have to cut anything; you can just add.'

'I'll jolly well add some humour,' said Miss Tibbs. 'It's as dull as ditchwater. Mind you, they're well cast.' She looked round at the actors appraisingly.

'Madeleine,' said Morgan Evans, 'you sound a little too flippant at times. I don't think Mr Stanley would like it. Remember, the magazine's frightfully hands-across-the-sea, if you understand me. Just a little more empire building, if you can manage it. Don't worry about it being too heavy. Miss Tibbs will see to that. Let's read it again, shall we? I don't think it's any good walking through, if the script's to be rewritten. Sorry, Moyra, about all that chalking-out.'

He smiled at a large, freckled young woman in slacks, who had been crawling about on her knees, marking out patterns on the floor with the aid of a ruler and an impressive-looking plan.

'Doesn't matter,' said Moyra. 'It had to be done some time. Now, I only hope they don't scrub the floor before tomorrow.'

After they had read the sketch again and discussed various points, Morgan Evans said, 'Maddy, you went too far that time. I expected you to wave a Union Jack at any moment.'

Maddy giggled shamefacedly.

'Still, it's a relief to find a child who *can* overact,' he observed. 'Usually it's a case of having to bully a girl of your age in order to get anything out of her at all. But remember, you don't need to do as much for television.'

'Mr Manyweather said I'd seem to be leaping out of the screen and biting people,' said Maddy.

'Yes,' Morgan Evans agreed, 'an apt description. You will have to tone it down a bit. Well, I don't think there's any sense in going further this morning. I'm sorry about the script situation, but you saw how it happened. And so—I'll see you all tomorrow.'

Morgan Evans, his secretary, and Moyra, the assistant floor manager, and a young man called Guy, who was the floor manager, all hurried back to the office, where they said there were a hundred and one things to do. The rest of the cast adjourned to a nearby cake shop and proceeded to get to know each other. Maddy found them very friendly and not so different from the seniors at the Academy. They told her how lucky she was to be going all the way through the series.

'I know,' said Maddy. 'And it was only because another girl got appendicitis. She was much better than I am. More sort of—well—refined, I suppose. Mr Evans wouldn't have had to tell her to be more empire building.'

'She sounds revolting,' laughed Rita, tossing her long dark hair. 'I'm sure you'll be much more amusing—you and Miss Mackenzie.'

'Now, don't call me Miss, miss,' Sunny remonstrated. 'I ain't used to it. Sunny's my name...'

'And sunny your nature,' quipped one of the actors. 'I hope, Miss Tibbs, you'll give her some good lines.'

'Do I have to learn them all off by heart?' Sunny frowned. 'I ain't learned anything by heart since Abraham Lincoln's Gettysburg address.'

'Don't worry, you'll be all right,' said Miss Tibbs. 'You're a "natural" as they say. Which state do you hail from?'

'From the South ma'am,' said Sunny, putting on a deep Southern drawl. 'But I've worked all over the wide world.'

Soon Sunny and Miss Tibbs were off on a long travelogue of all the places they had visited, while the others listened, exceedingly impressed.

Suddenly Maddy noticed the time.

'Goodness, I must fly if I'm going to get lunch and not be late for lessons this afternoon. You don't know how lucky you are to be all grown up, and not have to go to school.'

'I'd rather go to school than go home and clean up my flat—which is what I must do,' yawned Rita.

'Come on, Sunny,' Maddy urged. 'You'd better make a show of seeing me back to the Academy—then I'll see you on to your bus.'

They left the café amid shouts of laughter.

'I'm having the nicest time I ever did have,' said Sunny happily. 'And to think that I'm going to act on that television. What my folks will say when they hear, I just don't know.'

Maddy realised that by her 'folks' she meant her employers and their family.

'They'll just about go mad; I guess the young 'uns 'll never believe it.'

'Until they see you,' added Maddy. 'Isn't it exciting and terrible that thousands and thousands of people are going to see us.'

When she got back to the Academy she could hardly eat her lunch in the canteen because so many people as well as Mrs Seymore wanted to hear what the first rehearsal had been like. She had to tell over and over again how it was that Sunny had become part of the show.

She was so excited by her first day's rehearsal that she talked about it to Mrs Bosham and Zillah all the evening, and then dreamt about it all night.

She woke early, and wished it were time to get up and study her part, but knew that it was not really worthwhile, as the whole script would be changed by today.

At last it was time to go to rehearsal. She felt that she had settled in well enough to be able to wear slacks today.

Sunny joined her outside the Academy and they hurried through to Russell Square.

Miss Tibbs was buzzing about in the rehearsal room with some loose bits of paper, showing people where these were to be inserted in the scripts.

'It wasn't necessary to have the whole script redone,' she explained, 'only these little alterations.'

It made the script very difficult to follow, and when it came to reading it through, poor Sunny did not know where she was. She had obviously never seen a play script before, let alone a television script with all the action down the left side and all the dialogue down the right. She read the wrong lines and couldn't see when it was her turn, so that Maddy had to nudge her. Some of the cast raised their eyebrows doubtfully, but Morgan Evans said encouragingly, 'It'll be fine when you know it by heart.'

'This acting business,' said Sunny naively, 'it ain't at all easy.'

She took everything in such good part that she even won over the eyebrow-raisers.

Next they walked through the patterns that Moyra had marked on the floor. Here Maddy was as lost as Sunny. She always had had more difficulty with her moves than with her lines, and now she was constantly finding herself walking through a wall—a chalk-line one—or standing on a camera marked on the floor. Morgan Evans displayed limitless patience.

'Don't worry, girls and boys,' he told them. 'This is only Tuesday. By Saturday it'll be altogether different.'

'Only three whole days—no, *half* days,' Maddy wailed in horror.

'My dear child, you've got time to learn *War and Peace* by Saturday if you really set your mind to it,' Morgan Evans told her. 'And this is only a little short sketch.'

Maddy could manage her long screeds of announcement and explanation quite well, because while doing them she only had to stand still on one spot.

'Don't worry,' Morgan Evans kept telling her. 'When you get into the studio it'll all seem clear as daylight to you. Anyway, the viewers aren't going to see next Saturday's performance, and you'll have got over the worst by the time they actually see you.'

That evening Sunny went round to Fitzherbert Street, and they went through their lines together. Miss Tibbs had certainly come up to scratch and had given Sunny some very good lines, but Sunny had no idea of how to learn a part, and Maddy found herself trying to teach her the rudiments of drama, as they went along. In doing so she found that she had learnt a lot herself, and it was very late indeed when Mrs Bosham brought them up some cocoa, and insisted on Maddy going to bed.

'My folks will think I'm lost, Miss Maddy,' said Sunny between gulps of cocoa. 'I sure must run.' And down the stairs she hurried.

The next day's rehearsal was much better. It seemed somehow as if everything had fallen into place overnight. Sunny was still a little bit behind everyone else, which was only to be expected, as she had never acted in her life before.

The press cameramen who were supposed to have come on the Monday now turned up. And by this time everyone was really in working clothes with a vengeance—jeans and head scarves and everything. Sunny had her hair tied up in a large turban. The photographers were thrilled with her, and she quite stole the limelight, though Maddy came in for a good share of it.

When the photographers had gone, Morgan Evans heaved a sigh of relief.

'Now, let's get on with it. Through it again, please, and watch your cues. It's still very rough. And Maddy, try and mean what you say, and stop trying to make other people giggle.'

Maddy looked very grave.

'I'm sorry,' she said. 'Somehow it just seems to come over me.'

'Well, if you do it in the studio on Saturday something will come over Mr Stanley—an apoplectic fit, I should think. This show has got to be good—there's an option clause in your contract, you know.'

Maddy didn't know, because she had not seen the contract, which had gone direct to her father to be signed. But she gathered that Morgan Evans meant that if she were no good on Saturday they could throw her out. So she pulled up her socks and tried not to get the giggles, but it was very difficult with Sunny about.

All the cast had been for wardrobe fittings for their costumes, with the exception of Maddy and Sunny who were told to wear their own clothes. 'Bright summer dresses,' said Morgan Evans, 'but not too white.'

'Can I wear the same all the way through?' asked Maddy.

'No, I should change for the sketch, if you can make it. There'll be plenty of time during the dancing.'

'S'posing I get a zip stuck, or something,' said Maddy, alarmed.

'Don't worry, you'll have a dresser to help you.'

'Shall I really? Goodness, how important I'm getting,' said Maddy.

As Saturday approached, Morgan Evans began to work the cast like slaves. He stood in front of them, and more or less conducted—waving his arms and gesticulating at them to give more life, more speed—or whatever he thought was required. Once Sunny had mastered her lines she improved beyond measure.

'There,' cried Miss Tibbs, 'I told you she was a "natural".'

At the end of the Friday rehearsal Morgan Evans said, 'Well, that's all we can do. Once we get into the studios there will be so many technical considerations we shan't have time to do any polishing up on performances. Maddy, go to bed early. You look tired. With those circles under your eyes you'll look like a little panda on the screen. See you all at crack of dawn tomorrow—in costume and make-up by nine-thirty.'

Maddy was so far removed from her lessons that afternoon that she was twice reprimanded and threatened with being sent to Mrs Seymore. When school was over everyone crowded round to wish her luck.

'I do wish tomorrow's show was actually going *on*,' said Snooks. 'I want to *see* you...'

'Oh well, you'll only have to wait another week for the grand première,' joked Maddy. 'Don't miss it. Madeleine Fayne, the only acting panda in captivity. That's what the producer said I looked like this morning.'

Zillah could tell from Maddy's manner that she was extremely worried, so insisted on treating her to the cinema to take her mind off it, but as the film they saw was all about commercial radio shows in America it didn't really help much.

'I am sorry, I didn't know that was what it was about,' said Zillah as they walked home.

'Doesn't matter,' said Maddy. 'I'm afraid I didn't take in much of what was going on.'

The lines of the script had been running through her head throughout the entire performance. And when she went to bed she didn't think she would be able to sleep. But she did, and was quite surprised when she woke up to find Mrs Bosham standing by the bed with a cup of tea.

'As it's a special occasion...'

Poor Sunny was in quite a state of nerves when they met outside the Academy, and kept plying Maddy with questions about what it would be like.

'And these cameras, now. How big are they? Like a movie camera?'

'No,' said Maddy. 'Enormous—on wheels with two men riding on them.'

'Two men on them!'

'And the mikes are on another monstrosity on wheels,' said Maddy. 'I can't explain. But you'll see. Don't be surprised at anything!'

'Oh, mercy me,' wailed Sunny. 'I don't know how I came to be doing this at all.'

They cheered up a little when they reached the studios and were given the key to a small, neat dressing-room that had enormous mirrors on the walls with bright electric lights all round.

Having unpacked their cases and hung up their clothes they wondered what they ought to do next.

'P'raps we'd better change,' said Maddy.

While they were changing there was a knock at the door.

'Calling Miss Fayne and Miss Mackenzie,' shouted a voice.

'Ooh,' squealed Maddy, 'we're not made up.'

She peered round the door at a young man who was studying a list.

'You two aren't down for make-up,' he said. 'It isn't necessary.'

'Oh, what a shame,' wailed Maddy. 'I did want to be made up. Which is the way to the studio?'

'Come with me; I'll show you,' said the young man, and set off at such a rate that Maddy had to trot to keep up with him.

'Oh dear, I haven't got my script—did I remember to put on clean socks?—oh, where's my hankie?'

At each step Maddy kept remembering something she had forgotten.

When they entered the studio Sunny stopped dead in amazement.

'My, my, what a conglomeration!' she cried.

Conglomeration was the perfect word for it. In front of them were the actual settings which in the rehearsal room had only been indicated by chalk lines or represented by chairs; and there was so much equipment and so many cameras and booms that it seemed impossible to move.

'I'm done sure I'll never find my way around!' exclaimed Sunny.

'Oh, yes, you will,' said Maddy. 'Here, let's have a look at the sets first of all.'

The rest of the cast, wearing darkish make-up, were also exploring the sets, trying doors to see if they opened and shut properly, leaning against tree trunks to make sure they would not fall over.

There was considerable activity around the cameras, most of which seemed to be in pieces, having their insides checked over. Suddenly Morgan Evans appeared in the studio, looking very spruce and energetic.

'Have you discovered your announcement set, Maddy?' he asked.

'Er—no, not yet.' Maddy looked round wildly.

'It's in the same position as it was in the rehearsal room,' he told her.

'Yes, but everything looks different. Oh, is that it?'

'Yes, that's right. Would you mind getting over into it, so that the camera can get lined up on you. We'll try and run straight through, but if we have to stop occasionally to check things, don't be surprised. Remember that we really have got the dancers and changes today.'

'Oh, have we? Yes, of course,' said Maddy. She went over to a plain draped backing, with a table and chair in front of it, and sat down.

9

MADEMOISELLE X

The rest of that day was the most nerve-wracking Maddy had ever spent. Despite Morgan Evans's announcement that they would 'run straight through' they stopped and started continually. Maddy made three false starts on her opening speech. The first time she was using too much voice, the second time she was stopped for her chair to be moved a fraction of an inch to the right. And on the third occasion one of the dancers walked right across the front of the camera that was focused on Maddy.

It seemed as though they would never get as far as the sketch. The dancers and singers had been rehearsed separately by Morgan Evans's assistant, and this was the first time that the producer had seen them. All sorts of things seemed to be wrong with them, and Morgan Evans came down from the control room to the studio floor and put them through their paces.

Maddy was longing to go and watch, but did not dare leave her little bit of set. She had not been able to rehearse the interview properly, for the girl and boy who were to be interviewed were not arriving until the afternoon. By the middle of the morning she was ravenous, and could not imagine how she was going to last out until lunch-time. The lights were so hot that she felt much too warm, even in a summer dress.

The actors in the sketch sat about in bored attitudes, wondering when their calls would come and watching Maddy with, what seemed to her, coldly critical eyes.

The amount of activity in the studio was fantastic. The heavy cameras tracked silently into position and swarms of technicians walked about, stood and stared, adjusted lights, argued with each other, and one even came and held some sort of meter right under Maddy's nose, so that she sniffed at it and said, 'Delicious.'

He did not seem at all amused, however, and she felt rather silly. By lunch-time they still had not got as far as the sketch, and when they were told to break for an hour Sunny came up to Maddy and said, 'My stomach keeps doing the somersaults. I sure wish they'd get on with things.'

They went out to the restaurant where Maddy had had coffee the first time she had come to see Morgan Evans, but by now they were no longer hungry, and only toyed with their food.

'I can't see how we shall ever be ready to go on,' wailed Maddy. 'We haven't rehearsed the interviews or the sketch, and we go on at five. And I know I'm terrible. I can tell from the way people are watching me. And the sponsors won't like me. And I'll get the sack. Oh, how awful! I shall never be able to hold up my head at the Academy again.'

'It's all right for you, Miss Maddy,' Sunny told her. 'You been taught this acting, but I ain't never tried before.'

When they returned to the studio things seemed much more organised.

They started off with the sketch, which went quite well, although there were many stops and starts. Sunny was a big hit and made the studio staff laugh several times.

'Doesn't it seem tragic,' said Maddy to Rita, 'that all this trouble is being taken, and no one is going to see it except a few silly, fat old men.'

'Yes,' said Rita shrewdly, 'but if they like us, we're in, and if they don't—we're not.'

'Will the first programme that really goes on be the same as this one, do you think?'

Rita shrugged.

'Don't know,' she said. 'It all depends on Them.'

'Maddy,' yelled the floor manager in the distance. 'Madeleine Fayne, please.'

And Maddy realised that she had missed her cue for the closing announcement.

'You've got to be nippy here,' the floor manager told her. 'After you exit at the end of the sketch you've got to hurry round here, behind the scenery, and change in the quick-change room, then back into your own little set, and you've only got a minute and a half. Now, do you think you can do it?'

'Oh, yes,' said Maddy confidently. 'It's just that I forgot altogether this time. And it won't matter if my buttons aren't done up properly down the back, will it?'

'No,' laughed the floor manager, 'as long as your dress hangs on you, that's all that matters.'

Just then the call-boy came up to the floor manager and said, 'The girl and the boy for the interview have arrived. Shall I bring them up? Do they want make-up?'

'Yes, bring them up,' said the floor manager. 'Before we decide about make-up we'd better see them on the tube,' meaning on the television screen.

Maddy was greatly relieved to hear that the boy and girl had arrived, and that she would have an opportunity to rehearse with them. To her surprise they both greeted her in excellent English, shaking hands politely.

The French boy was very small for his age, and extremely serious. He was accompanied by a fierce-looking man, who gabbled away angrily at him in French every few minutes.

The Persian girl was about sixteen, and quite attractive, with lovely limpid eyes, but rather a long nose. Maddy found the interview extremely difficult. She had learnt the questions she was to ask, but the girl and the boy constantly anticipated them, so that by the time Maddy got to a certain question it had already been answered. The most difficult thing was to bring the interviews to a close gracefully. At first both the boy and the girl were shy, but by the end of the conversation they were in full swing. The first time she went through with the girl, Maddy saw the floor manager making 'Cut' gestures by drawing the side of his hand across his throat, and she said firmly, 'Oh, we've got to stop now. Sorry.'

Everyone laughed, and Morgan Evans came down into the studio and said quite kindly, 'No, Maddy, you mustn't finish it off like that. If you've got to stop abruptly just say very firmly, "Well, thank you very much, so-and-so, for coming along to the studio today. We've certainly learnt a lot about your country"—something like that. But never, "We've got to stop now."'

'Sorry,' said Maddy. 'From the faces that the floor manager was making I thought it must be urgent.'

At last they were able to get a run through the whole show, and everyone began to feel better about it. Morgan Evans came down from the control room with a sheaf of notes on their performances.

'Don't grin so much, Maddy. Rita, don't sway when you're in close-up. You keep up a constant roll as though you were on board ship. You'll make everybody seasick. The dancers must hold their pose at the end until we've faded. Some of them moved'—and so on for a long time.

Then he said, 'And now *The World of Youth* editorial board want to see you all at tea in Room Fifty. If you'll follow me.'

When Maddy saw the tea that was laid out on a long table she gave a wail of dismay.

'Oh, no! Not *before* the show! I just couldn't. Meringues! And I can't touch one.'

She was so deeply upset by this bad bit of planning that she went up to Mr Stanley of *The World of Youth* and said earnestly, 'Do you think they'll clear all this away while we're doing the programme?'

'I expect so,' said Mr Stanley. 'We shall be having a conference after the show.'

'Oh, what a shame,' said Maddy. 'You see, my tummy is so full of butterflies at the moment I haven't got any room even for a meringue, and I was wondering whether I could come back here afterwards and make up for it.'

Mr Stanley smiled indulgently.

'I'll see to it that a special plate of cakes is reserved for you until after the show,' he promised.

'Oh, thank you, that's very kind of you,' said Maddy gratefully, and went in search of a cup of tea and a dry biscuit.

Everyone seemed in much the same state of excitement and the tea was hardly touched.

'We'll have the whole spread left till after the show,' said Morgan Evans. 'You won't mind if we eat while we talk at the conference, will you?'

'Not at all,' said Mr Stanley. 'I'm hoping there won't be a great deal to be said.'

All too soon the call-boy came knocking at the door, to take the cast down to have their make-up touched up. To Maddy's delight she had her face powdered, and her lashes and eyebrows darkened a little. Sunny's face was powdered too, with the darkest powder they could find, for under the lights her skin was apt to shine as though it had been polished.

As they made their way back to the studio Maddy kept saying, 'After all, nobody's going to *see* this programme. It's not going *out*.'

'Then why are we doing it?' demanded Sunny, who had never really understood the whole situation.

'Because it will be so nice when it's over!' laughed Rita, looking very glamorous in her costume and exotic make-up.

Morgan Evans came round giving last words of advice.

'Lots of sincerity, Maddy. Not too much grinning. And for heaven's sake don't forget that last quick change.'

While she was waiting for her cue Maddy felt very conscious of all the important people sitting in front of the television screen up in Room 50.

'Well, if they don't like it, they'll have to lump it,' she thought, just as the floor manager gave her the signal to start.

Of course her first grin was too wide, and the interviews were rather slow and over-ran slightly, but the quick changes went beautifully with the help of a dresser, and Maddy knew that the sketch was good. But during her quick change back for the final announcement, there was nearly a tragedy. Some of the hair at the end of Maddy's left plait got twisted round a button, and there she was, inextricably caught up, with the seconds ticking by.

'Now, don't squeal,' ordered the dresser, a motherly woman with spectacles, and she gave a brisk tug that pulled the hairs out at the roots.

Maddy didn't squeal, but the tears sprang to her eyes and caused her mascara to run. She made the last announcement with tears rolling down her cheeks.

And then it was all over, and the floor manager was waving his arms and saying, 'Relax, everyone, relax.'

Morgan Evans came down into the studio carrying a sheaf of notes as usual, saying, 'Pretty good, everyone. Not bad at all. Now, go and change and come up to Room Fifty and we'll hear the worst.'

'You were jolly good, Sunny,' said Maddy. 'They *must* have liked you.'

'I'm just about on my knees,' laughed Sunny. 'I ain't never been so tired in all my born days.'

They splashed cold water over their faces in an effort to cool down, and then, tremblingly, made their way up to Room 50, where Mr Stanley greeted them at the door.

'Very nice, Madeleine. Very nice, Miss Mackenzie. I knew I'd spotted a winner.'

He was beaming with pride, as though he had acted the part himself, and not Sunny.

'And now, we have one or two suggestions to make, haven't we, gentlemen?'

The one or two suggestions turned out to be a complete remoulding of the whole programme. Miss Tibbs was there with her notebook and pencil saying, 'Yes, yes' in a business-like way to every suggestion that was made. The only difficulty was that many of the suggestions were completely impracticable.

Morgan Evans pointed these out as patiently as he could, saying, 'You see, if we move the singing and the dancing from the middle of the programme to the beginning, it means Maddy has no time to change before the sketch...'

'But *must* she change?' asked one of the board.

'We think it helps the illusion a little,' said Morgan Evans. 'If she's wearing the same dress as she was wearing in the studio scenes the viewers are less likely to believe that she's in South America.'

'True, true,' said Mr Stanley. 'But isn't there some other way to get round it?'

Maddy, on her third meringue, could see that it was going to be a long session. They rambled on and on, occasionally coming back to a point that they all agreed on, such as, 'And Maddy, you must appear to take it more seriously. It's no good looking as though the whole thing is a huge joke. If you could compère the show as earnestly as you're getting through that plate of cakes, it would be a good thing. But it was a jolly good effort, and you remembered every point we told you.'

'And so can I do the series?' asked Maddy point-blank.

'What's that?'

'You mean you're not throwing me out.'

Mr Stanley threw up his hands in horror. 'No, no, no. My dear child, what an idea—of course not. You and Miss Mackenzie will appear in the whole series, as contracted. And we hope to include the other artistes from time to time. Now, Miss Tibbs, as to next week's script...'

It was nearly half past six and the show had finished at half past five, when Morgan Evans interrupted Mr Stanley with, 'Don't you think the cast could go home? We've got a great deal to decide before rehearsal on Monday. They've had a hard day of it, I know.'

'Oh, yes, by all means. Run along,' said Mr Stanley. 'You've made a good try of it, everyone. But there are a lot of ends to be tied up by this time next week.'

The editorial board beamed and shook hands as the cast went out, and once in the street Maddy turned to Sunny and said, 'We're really going to be on television! I never thought it would happen.'

The Monday rehearsal began a week of turmoil. The whole script had been rewritten once more, so that it bore only a slight resemblance to the first one, and this made it extremely difficult to learn.

The musical part of the programme was to be totally different and the same boy was to be interviewed, but not the same girl. Poor Rita's part had been cut to nothing, as the editorial board had considered that she was 'too glamorous' to fit in with the tone of the programme.

'Not very flattering to Sunny and me,' giggled Maddy.

But when she read some of the copies of *The World of Youth* that Mr Stanley had insisted on sending her, she saw what they meant. The tone of the whole magazine was more earnest and 'hands-across-the-sea-ish' than Rita could ever be—and certainly than Maddy herself.

The week seemed to fly, and by the weekend everyone was exhausted and rather fed up with learning variations of the same script.

Maddy was not so frightened this week, although she knew the programme was to be seen by millions of viewers. She was used to a large audience, but the thought of a few important gentlemen sitting up in a viewing room was much worse.

The pace of things at the Academy was increasing too, for the end-of-term shows were looming near. Fortunately, Maddy had only been given small parts because of her television work, but Zillah was playing the lead in a detective play, in which she had the role of a beautiful spy, and had to speak with a foreign accent. This she had learnt syllable by syllable from Armand, the French boy in their class, who was himself playing an English colonel with great difficulty.

The entire Academy had promised to watch Maddy on Saturday afternoon, and her mother had phoned to say that they had had a set installed for the same purpose. There was to be a large gathering at Mrs Bosham's, another at Snooks's house and another in the common room at the Academy. Everyone wished Maddy luck on Friday evening, and loaded her with mascots of every type.

'I can't take them all to the studio,' said Maddy to Zillah. 'I think perhaps I'll leave them at home and just take Disgusting.'

'Disgusting' was the remains of a teddy bear that she had had from infancy, which was now scarcely recognisable, but which went with her on very special occasions, even if it meant doing him up in a brown-paper parcel to disguise him.

On Saturday morning there were telegrams from her mother and father, and Sandra and the rest of the Blue Doors, saying that they would be watching, and wishing her luck; and one from Mr Manyweather saying, 'Best of luck to my prize pupil'.

Mrs Bosham was busy preparing a fine spread for the friends that Zillah was bringing to watch.

'Leave some for me!' begged Maddy. 'I shall be ravenous when I come in, because I don't suppose they'll give us tea again this week.'

She went off to the studio in quite a festive mood, and Sunny was just as excited.

'My folks is having a party,' she told Maddy, 'and all the young 'uns is asking their friends in. My, my, I'd better be good.'

The studio did not seem so frightening this week, and it was nice to be greeted by name by the call-boy and the camera crew. The rehearsal was as chaotic as ever, but Maddy now realised that this was normal and nothing to worry about.

Nobody seemed quite as tense this week. As Morgan Evans said, 'There's no point in worrying now. They'll either like us, or they won't.'

At lunch-time there were more press photographers, and much posing for photographs all over the studio.

Maddy had one taken sitting on a camera, which delighted her, and Sunny and Morgan Evans had one taken 'conferring over the script'.

The afternoon rehearsal was quite smooth, and Maddy found the Chinese girl she had to interview much easier than the Persian of the previous week. But in the sketch everybody started reverting to last week's lines, and Rita got herself absolutely tied up and had to be prompted.

'You'll be all right,' Morgan Evans comforted her. 'It's just that being in the studio again brings back the lines you said when you were here last.'

At tea-time Sunny and Maddy just sat in their dressing-room and drank some milk and ate biscuits that Mrs Bosham had made Maddy bring.

Just before the programme was due to start the call-boy knocked on the door, and came in bearing two beautiful bouquets, one for Maddy and one for Sunny, each bearing the same message, 'Good wishes for your first television appearance. I know you'll be good.' They were signed 'Morgan Evans'.

This quite made the day for them both.

'Flowers,' cried Maddy. 'Just as though I were grown-up.'

'Flowers,' cried Sunny. 'Just as though I was'—she hesitated, then finished up—'a real actress.'

Maddy was so thrilled that she did not feel any butterflies in her tummy when the call-boy cried, 'On the set, please.'

It was not until she sat waiting for the floor manager's signal that she suddenly realised that in a few seconds millions of people sitting at their tea would be saying, 'Oh, who's this? What a funny girl!' and so on.

But it was too late to worry; the red light had gone on on the camera in front of her and the floor manager's arm had fallen—the signal to begin.

'Smooth as silk,' cried Morgan Evans afterwards, kissing her on both cheeks. 'And you really looked as though you meant it all. No Cheshire grins. Jolly good.'

'I say,' said Maddy, 'thank you for the flowers.'

The editorial board came down into the studio, delighted with it all, quite sure that the alterations they had recommended had made the show.

'Isn't it heavenly when it's over,' cried Maddy, as they took off their make-up.

But the day was not over, by any means. As Maddy and Sunny passed the Academy on the way home, a group of students who had been watching the programme rushed out to congratulate them, and insisted on taking them to an ice-cream parlour and buying them enormous sundaes.

Back at Mrs Bosham's a gang of the 'Babies', replete after a huge tea, were loud in their praise too. Zillah, shining-eyed, said to Maddy. 'You looked just like you, only *serious*!'

'I *was* serious,' laughed Maddy. 'I knew all you critical creatures were watching me.'

The next few weeks flew by, bringing the last week of term. Maddy was quite relieved to think that she could soon devote her energies entirely to television, for she was in such a whirl that she hardly had time to think.

The reaction to the first programme was favourable, and Morgan Evans was delighted with them all. Maddy and Sunny each had several fan letters, which thrilled them considerably, and they answered them with care.

'We're doing very nicely,' said Morgan Evans. 'If we can keep the programme up to standard for the next couple of weeks we shall have nothing to worry about.'

But on the Saturday before the end of term everything began to go wrong.

Maddy woke up with a bad cold, there was a go-slow strike of studio electricians, and bad weather delayed the plane on which one of the children to be interviewed was to travel.

At four o'clock Morgan Evans was tearing his hair and muttering in Welsh.

'We must just *find* someone,' he cried. 'Have we got anyone in the studios? Any colonials perhaps?'

Strangely enough, there was neither a foreigner nor a colonial available.

'We'll just have to go out into the street and *find* someone,' cried Morgan Evans, turning round to look for his assistant. Then suddenly he seemed to remember something, and turned back to Maddy.

'What about that friend of yours?' he asked. 'She's a central European of some sort...'

'Central European?' Maddy looked puzzled.

'Yes, you know the one. You brought her with you the second time you came to see me—you said she didn't speak very much English.'

Maddy suddenly realised who he meant.

'Oh, her!'

'Yes. Can you get hold of her—at once?'

'Well—er—yes,' stammered Maddy. 'I *can*, but...'

'There's no time to argue about it,' said Morgan Evans. 'Go and ring her. If you can't get her we'll just have to search the highways and byways.'

Maddy struggled to get out the right words, but Morgan Evans barked at her quite crossly. 'Go *on*! Tell her we'll pay her, but it'll all have to be arranged afterwards. There's no time to do anything but get her here *now*. Now, now, *now*—do you understand?'

'All right,' said Maddy. 'If you're sure you want her.' And she ran off to the telephone, giggling quietly to herself.

She knew that Zillah would be at home, because every week religiously she watched the programme in Mrs Bosham's basement.

With her hand cupped round the mouthpiece, Maddy said urgently when Zillah answered, 'Listen, it's Maddy here. Come round to the studios at once. Morgan Evans wants you in the programme.'

'Me?'

'Yes. Someone's let us down. And Morgan Evans thought of you. He thinks you're foreign because I said you couldn't speak very good English.'

'But—but where does he think I come from?'

'I don't know—central Europe, he said, or something.'

'But—but what have I got to do?' cried Zillah, horrified.

'Just be interviewed by me. And you can speak with the accent you are using in the play.'

'Oh, Maddy! No, I couldn't.'

'Yes, of course you could,' said Maddy firmly. 'Put on your green dress, get a taxi and come round right away. You'll be paid, so you can afford one. Now don't let me down.'

She rang off before Zillah could say no, but was by no means certain that she would come.

'She was very doubtful about it all,' Maddy reported to Morgan Evans. 'But I think she's coming.'

'Oh, thank heavens. What's her name? Something unpronounceable? Oh well, we'll have to get all the details after the programme. Just ask her the usual questions, and if she gets in a muddle answer for her. You know the routine. I hope she gets here in time for lighting and make-up to see her.'

Maddy was feeling a little light in the head from her cold, and could not really appreciate the seriousness of what she was about to do. Zillah arrived breathless and very upset, a quarter of an hour before the programme began.

There was only just time for the make-up department to powder her face and comb her hair, and the camera to line up on her, and Morgan Evans to say, 'Oh, I am glad you're here, Miss—er—Now don't be frightened, will you? Just answer the questions that Maddy asks you.'

Zillah nodded shyly, and then it was time for Morgan Evans to go up into the control room. Zillah was the first item on the programme, so there was no time for her to do more than whisper agonisedly to Maddy, 'But I shall have to tell some awful lies.'

'No,' said Maddy. 'Tell the truth. It'll sound all right in that accent.'

It was perfectly true. It did sound convincing in Zillah's strange half-French, half-West-Country accent. As she spoke of the village and the school at Polgarth one visualised somewhere in mid-Europe.

Maddy cleverly refrained from stating outright where the guest had come from, and kept to such questions as, 'And so you had never seen television till you came to London?'

'No,' replied Zillah. 'Nor the theatre or the cinema.'

When Maddy had exhausted all the safe questions she was horrified to see that the floor manager had chalked up on a blackboard in large capitals, 'WHERE DOES SHE COME FROM?'

Morgan Evans, up in the control room, was obviously frantic, because they had neglected to name Zillah's home. There was only one thing for it.

'And where exactly do you come from?' asked Maddy formally.

Zillah looked at her reproachfully, and said in an even more broken accent:

'Polgarth.'

As she said it Maddy sneezed loudly, so that the name was totally unintelligible. After that, she felt so pleased with herself she could not keep a Cheshire-cat grin from spreading over her face.

When the interview was over poor Zillah was trembling from head to foot, and nearly in tears of nervousness.

'That was terrific,' Maddy whispered to her during the musical interlude. 'Nothing to worry about.'

The sketch went very well, apart from Maddy getting a strangled sneeze that held up the action for a few seconds, and then went away again. And by the end of the programme Maddy was quite sure they had got away with it. But after the last fade-out, when they were all standing around the studio chatting happily, Morgan Evans appeared with a face like thunder. He walked straight up to Maddy and towered over her.

'I have just received a long-distance call from the West Country,' he said. 'And it would appear that your friend is a native of the village of Polgarth in Cornwall, and the girl is as English as you are. You are suspended from the programme, Madeleine, until further notice.'

10

BASIL

There was silence in the studio for some seconds, and then Maddy burst into loud sobs. Sunny hurried up to comfort her, and Zillah vainly tried to make some kind of explanation to Morgan Evans.

'It's not you I'm cross with,' said Morgan Evans. 'I don't know who you are or where you've come from. You gave a very good performance. There's no reason why you should be concerned about the show as a whole, but Maddy should have known better.'

'But I...'

'I don't want to hear any more.'

And he strode out of the studio.

'Come along, honey. Just you come down to the dressing-room with Sunny. You didn't mean no harm. We all know that.'

On the way to the dressing-room Maddy could not control her tears. They gushed unchecked as Zillah and Sunny led her along the corridors.

'Suspended from the programme,' she wailed, when they were in the dressing-room. 'Oh, how terrible! Whatever shall I do? Whatever will Mummy and Daddy say? And everyone at the Academy. And the Blue Doors.'

And she went off into fresh paroxysms.

'I'm so sorry,' said Zillah miserably. 'It's all because of me.'

'It's not your fault; it's all mine,' said Maddy, sniffing and trying to mop her face with a sodden handkerchief.

'I knew I ought not to do it. But I didn't realise it was as serious as it seems now.'

'It's that Morgan Evans's own fault,' maintained Sunny stoutly. 'I heard him tell you go fetch Miss Zillah. I heard him clear as a bell. And you tried to explain, and he wouldn't listen. Why, he nearly bit your head off.'

'Yes,' hiccupped Maddy. 'So I thought, "Well, if that's how you feel, you can jolly well have her." I never thought it would lead to serious trouble.'

'I wonder who it was rang up from home,' marvelled Zillah. 'Just fancy, they could see me as far away as Polgarth.'

'Oh dear,' sniffed Maddy. 'I hope it won't get you into trouble as well, Zillah.'

'If my father gets to hear about it he'll be angry with me pretending to be something I'm not. "That's where this play acting gets you," he'll say.'

They sat glumly about the dressing-room, without the heart to get changed. Maddy kept hoping there would be some message from Morgan Evans, but nothing happened. So eventually they packed up their things and left the building.

'But what will happen on Monday?' demanded Maddy. 'Will he have got someone else in time for the rehearsal?

Sunny, you will ring me up and let me know what happens—what he says, and everything.'

'Of course, honey. But you will have heard something by then. Just you see. Now don't you fret—neither of you. It'll all turn out all right.'

Despite Sunny's comforting assurances Maddy and Zillah were very despondent as they walked through the sunlit evening to Fitzherbert Street.

Mrs Bosham greeted them with, 'Well, I *was* proud of the pair of you.'

But when she saw their faces she stopped.

'Why, whatever's up?'

'I've been expelled,' Maddy burst out. 'I mean—suspended.' And once more she was in floods of tears. Zillah tried to explain the whole sad story, but it did not make much sense to Mrs Bosham.

'Well, of all the ingratitude!' she said indignantly. 'Why, you'd've thought he'd've been glad you came to the rescue, Zillah. And nobody would've *known* you weren't a foreigner. Really they wouldn't.'

'There was a phone call from my village,' explained Zillah. 'Someone who recognised me.'

'Oh, what hard lines,' said Mrs Bosham. 'Still, why blame Maddy?'

'It was all my fault. Everything always is. It's just like my mother says—I'm my own worst enemy,' said Maddy pathetically. 'I think I'll go to bed now. But let me know if there's a phone call.'

'What, go to bed without your supper?' cried Mrs Bosham, horrified.

'Yes,' said Maddy, and went out of the room.

Mrs Bosham shook her head wonderingly. 'That's the first time I've ever known her to miss a meal. Things must be bad.'

Maddy lay in bed stiff as a board and far from sleep, with her ears strained for the sound of the telephone. It rang several times during the evening, but always for one of the other lodgers. When Zillah came up to bed Maddy's eyes were still wide open. Zillah crept quietly into bed without saying a word and turned out the light, but it was very late before either of them fell asleep.

Sunday was the most miserable day Maddy had ever spent. She would not stir from the house in case the telephone rang, and her ears began to ache with imagining the sound of telephone bells. Slowly the enormity of what she had done began to dawn on her. She started to feel less sorry for herself, but more guilty.

'It was a dreadful thing to do,' she said to Zillah. 'Suppose Morgan Evans gets into terrible trouble over it and loses his job?'

'I shouldn't think he would,' said Zillah comfortingly. 'I mean—why should they blame him?'

'For not checking up on you first,' said Maddy.

'But it was all so sudden.'

'I don't suppose that Mr Stanley and all those other penguin-like men would realise that,' said Maddy gloomily. Then suddenly her face brightened.

'I know what,' she cried. 'I know what I'll do.'

'What? What?' asked Zillah.

'I'll go and see Mr Stanley, and explain to him exactly how it happened. I think *he* might listen. Morgan Evans is too cross at the moment.'

'When will you go?' asked Zillah fearfully.

'Tomorrow morning,' said Maddy with determination. 'As soon as the office is open. In fact I'll be waiting on the doorstep for him.'

'But where—where is his doorstep?—I mean his office?' demanded Zillah.

'I'll find it all right,' said Maddy. 'I'll look in those magazines he gave me. There's sure to be an address somewhere.'

There was. It gave the name of a street off the Strand.

'Right,' said Maddy, quite cheerful now that her mind was made up. 'I'll be there first thing tomorrow morning. Come on, let's go out for a walk. I don't particularly want to talk to Morgan Evans now, even if he does ring.'

They went out for a stroll and from a barrow bought some monkey nuts, which they ate all the way home, leaving a trail of shells behind them. Maddy chatted about everything under the sun except television, and Zillah marvelled at the speed with which her moods changed.

When they got in Mrs Bosham said, 'That Merryheather phoned. Seemed terrible upset. He'd heard about you, Maddy, and was wondering if you were all right. I said you was and you wasn't.'

'Oh dear,' said Maddy. 'I expect he'll be furious with me.'

'He didn't sound it—just sorry. He said he'd see you at the Academy tomorrow, because he's got a class.'

'I shan't be there till late,' said Maddy. 'I've got an important appointment.'

Sure enough on Monday morning, before the office of *The World of Youth* opened, Maddy was sitting on the doorstep.

The first person to arrive was not, as Maddy had expected, Mr Stanley himself, but the office boy.

'What you doin' there, Blondie?' he demanded.

Maddy stood up and drew herself to her full four feet something and replied, 'I wish to see Mr Stanley.'

'You'll be lucky, at this hour,' was the reply. 'Never gets 'ere before ten. Otherwise, what's the use of being the boss?'

'Oh well, can I come in and wait?' asked Maddy.

'S'pose so,' said the boy rather grudgingly. 'Old Wilson the commissionaire will be here with the keys in a minute. He'll let us in, and you can tell him you know the boss. You're on this television lark, aren't you?'

'Yes, that's right,' said Maddy. 'How did you know?'

'I seen you,' was the reply.

'Did you see Saturday's show?' asked Maddy.

He nodded.

'I messed things up properly,' said Maddy. 'You know that girl—the foreign one—well, she isn't foreign at all. She's as English as I am. Isn't it awful? And it was all my fault. Mr Stanley's going to be furious. And I've been suspended from the show already.'

'Cor,' whistled the boy. 'Still, you don't want to worry about old Stan—he's as soft as they come. As long as you say you're sorry, he'll be all right.'

'Do you really think so?'

'Oh, yes. He's always saying, "Forgive and forget". It's one of his theme songs, so he jolly well ought to live up to it. Oh, here's old Wilson,' and he explained Maddy's presence to a tall genial-looking commissionaire who had joined them, swinging a bunch of keys.

Soon the boy and Maddy were in the general office of *The World of Youth*. It was very smart, with pale beige carpet, light-oak furniture and heavy velvet curtains. On the walls were pictures of children from different countries, wearing their national costumes.

The office boy immediately got busy filling ink wells and putting out fresh blotting paper. Maddy stood in the middle of the floor, not quite knowing what to do.

'Can I help you?' she asked.

'I've more or less finished in here,' he said. 'But you can take this blotting paper into old Stan's office, if you like, and throw away the used lot. That's his room.'

Mr Stanley's office was even more plushy than the outer one. Maddy was surprised to see on the walls publicity photographs of the television programme, including some of herself. She changed the blotting paper on the desk, and then noticed that there were some dead flowers in a vase on the bookcase. She threw them away in the waste-paper basket, and was standing holding the jug, wondering what to do with the dirty water, when the door suddenly swung open and Mr Stanley walked in.

Maddy was so startled that she dropped the jug on to the floor. The greenish-tinted water ran all over the pale carpet and the handle came off the jug.

Maddy looked down at the mess and murmured, 'Oh, Mr Stanley, I'm sorry—I—we didn't expect you so soon.'

'What on earth are you doing here?' said Mr Stanley. 'And just look at what you've done. From all accounts you've caused enough trouble, without coming here and pouring water all over my carpet.'

Maddy was nearly in tears of despair. It was a most unfortunate opening to the interview. Mr Stanley went to the door and shouted to the office boy, 'Basil, bring a cloth,' then sat down at his desk.

Maddy stood miserably by the pool on the carpet while Basil mopped it up, clicking his tongue in a disapproving fashion. Then he removed the jug and its handle.

Mr Stanley was looking very sternly at Maddy.

'Now, what's all this I've heard from Mr Morgan Evans? I watched the programme at home on Saturday, and thought it went very well, but Morgan Evans rang me up in the evening to tell me that he had discovered that one of the interviews was a hoax you had played, and that he had suspended you from the programme. I've not had a chance to find out any details about it, and that is why I have come here so early this morning—to try and sort things out. Now perhaps you can give me your version of what happened.'

Maddy took a deep breath and began. It was difficult to explain without appearing to be putting all the blame on the producer.

'And I tried to tell him that she wasn't foreign at all, and he wouldn't listen—I really tried hard...'

'Couldn't you have shouted out, "But she's English"?'

'I suppose I could,' said Maddy. 'But I wanted Zillah to have a chance on the programme.'

Mr Stanley sighed heavily.

'Oh, Maddy, it is very difficult to make you understand. I can see that you may have done it from motives of friendship, but if you were thinking of other people, why didn't you give a thought to Morgan Evans, and to me, and the

173

reputation of the programme and of the very magazine itself? You see, we have a name for dependability and sincerity, and if it becomes known that we had someone on the programme who was a—a phoney, it will absolutely ruin us. If the papers get hold of it they'll make a very amusing story out of it.'

'If I'm suspended from the programme,' said Maddy ponderingly, 'the papers may very well get hold of it.'

Mr Stanley looked at her sharply. 'Are you trying to blackmail me?' he demanded.

Maddy hastily changed her line. 'Oh, no, Mr Stanley,' she said earnestly. 'I'm just—hoping that you will forgive and forget.'

She opened her eyes very wide, and looked at him steadily. Mr Stanley returned the gaze, and finally he wilted. He was more impressed by the thought that it would look strange if Maddy were out of the programme, than by the plea for forgiveness. Thoughtfully he put the tips of his fingers together.

'Maddy,' he said importantly, 'I think that perhaps the producer has been a little rash in suspending you, and I am a firm believer in the maxim you have just mentioned, "Forgive and forget". If you will assure me that you will never do anything of the kind again I will overlook it this time. I will have a talk with Morgan Evans and see that you are reinstated in the programme. And you must not tell anyone else about all this, and your friend—Mademoiselle X, shall we say—must not talk about it either. That's most important. If an inquiry arises from people who know her true identity, we shall have to face up to it, and I hope you will realise the predicament in which you have placed us.'

'Oh, thank you, thank you,' Maddy cried. '*Dear* Mr Stanley, I knew it was the right thing to do, to come to you.'

Maddy was smiling for the first time in nearly two days, but her eyes had filled with tears of relief.

As she hurried through the office she startled Basil, the office boy, by throwing her arms round him saying, 'Thank you a thousand times for telling me about "Forgive and forget".'

Maddy ran all the way to the rehearsal room, arriving hot and untidy. She burst through the door, then stopped in sudden confusion. It had struck her that Morgan Evans might not be overjoyed to see her again—he might not believe that Mr Stanley had said everything was all right.

Morgan Evans detached himself from a group of actors and came over to Maddy. He looked down at her, half-angry, half-amused.

'So it's the prodigal,' he said.

'I—I've been to see Mr Stanley,' Maddy began.

'Yes, I know. He's just rung me. And it appears that we have got to "Forgive and forget".'

'That's right,' said Maddy. 'Do you think you can?'

Morgan Evans went rather red with some stifled emotion that Maddy could not quite recognise. It might have been anger, or again it might have been amusement.

'I'll do my best,' he said. 'If the boss's happy about it, then I am. But on Saturday I thought you'd lost me my job. Come on, now, we're late enough already. Let's get down to the read-through.'

Sunny and Miss Tibbs welcomed Maddy with open arms.

'Gee, was I worried!' Sunny whispered to her. 'They was

talking about getting another girl. But then that Mr Stanley phoned. He must be a real gentleman.'

'Oh, he is,' said Maddy. 'I should like to—to knit him a sweater.'

Considering that Maddy had never knitted anything more complicated than a doll's scarf, it was unlikely that she would ever carry out this threat.

She was so pleased to be back in the show that she put all the enthusiasm she could muster into the read-through, so that Morgan Evans had to tell her constantly not to overact. Nevertheless, he seemed cheerful, and in the coffee break he said to the cast, 'We've had the figures in for the first two shows, and they're excellent.'

'What figures?' Maddy wanted to know.

'The viewer-reaction figures. We make inquiries about how many people enjoyed what programmes, and the statistics arrived at are supposed to be representative.'

Maddy didn't quite understand all this, but gathered that he was pleased because the show was proving popular.

After the rehearsal she hurried back to the Academy, where the end-of-term shows were in progress. As she slipped into a seat in the theatre next to Zillah, watching some of the seniors performing *She Stoops to Conquer*, she whispered to her, 'It's all right. I'm back in the show. And all is forgiven and forgotten.'

'But what about me? Have they forgiven me too?'

'They never blamed you at all,' Maddy told her. 'I'll tell you about it afterwards.'

By Thursday all the shows were over and the pupils were ready to depart. Maddy was rather sorry to say goodbye to

Zillah, but Zillah was obviously looking forward to seeing her home again, though Maddy could not help feeling that the household sounded rather grim.

It would be something of a relief, really, not to have any more work at the Academy for a while, for now she could devote her whole attention to the *World of Youth* programme, and try to be so good that Morgan Evans really would forgive her.

On the Thursday afternoon Maddy went with Zillah to Paddington to see her off, and then returned to 'The Boshery' feeling rather lost, and wishing that there was a rehearsal to go to at once, instead of having to wait until the following morning.

Fortunately Sunny rang up, and asked her if she would care to go round for the evening, as her 'young 'uns' were longing to meet Maddy, and also they would be able to go over their lines together.

Maddy accepted with whoops of delight, but there was not much studying of lines done that evening. When Maddy arrived at the luxurious flat where Sunny's employers lived she found that the 'young 'uns' were an assortment of high-spirited American girls and boys, whose idea of a quiet evening at home was jiving to the radiogram, or playing 'Murders' all over the apartment.

Next day at rehearsal Morgan Evans arrived looking as if he were bursting with news. He and his secretary and assistant and Miss Tibbs kept having private chinwags in corners, and looking very pleased about something. Before they started work he lifted a hand for silence, and said, 'I have some news. You remember I told you right at the beginning of the series that the shape of the programme might change before the end. Well, the time has come to make a most important announcement. In the last programme of the series the sketch will not be done in the studio; it will be a filmed insert, taken in Paris.'

For a minute Maddy did not understand.

'You will have noticed that we have covered countries farthest away from England and have now nearly reached Europe. Well, when we get as close as France, Maddy and Sunny will actually be there, and will be filmed.'

There were gasps of delight from Maddy and Sunny, and of envy from the other artists.

'You mean—you mean we really *go* to Paris?' demanded Maddy.

'Yes, just for one night—if you're good, that is. But one false move, Miss Fayne, and you're out of it, understand? It's quite a different matter playing the giddy goat on your own home ground, but if you get up to your tricks abroad you really will be out on your neck. Is that clear?'

'Yes.'

Maddy tried to sound meek, but a grin of excitement spread from ear to ear.

'Of course, we'll have to get written permission from your parents, Maddy. It will mean travelling to Paris by plane, then a day's filming there before travelling back again to do the show. So it'll be pretty hectic.'

'By plane!' Maddy cried. 'I've never been in one.'

'Sunny, do you feel capable of chaperoning Maddy on the Continent, or would you prefer her mother to come too?'

'Just as you like, boss,' said Sunny. 'I 'spect I can manage her, but if she'd like her Momma to come along...'

'Miss Tibbs is coming too,' said Mr Morgan Evans. 'And my secretary and the camera crew, so between us we ought to be able to manage, I think.'

He smiled at Maddy in a way that made her think perhaps, after all, he had forgiven her for the Zillah incident, and she felt so happy that she could have burst.

'Paris...' she breathed to herself all the way through the rehearsal. It suddenly seemed very dull to be doing a sketch about a foreign land in a studio every week, and she could not wait to see a real foreign country and its real people instead of just settings and actors.

Now that they had all got into the swing of the programmes the time seemed to flash by. No sooner was one show over than it was time to start rehearsing the next. And as Maddy said one Saturday, 'It always seems to be transmission day.'

She became quite used to learning a new script each week and meeting new actors for the sketches, and different girls and boys for the interviews. She became quite good at coping with different moves from camera to camera, and when, during an interview, an African girl fainted from sheer excitement she handled the situation with perfect ease. She could see from the light on top of the cameras that just before the girl collapsed they had cut away to a map of Africa, showing where the girl came from, and so Maddy went on talking as she helped the floor manager to pick up the girl and take her off the set, saying, 'And on the map you can see just where Comfort Owo comes from. That's the town where she lives—marked with an arrow.'

Meanwhile the next person to be interviewed was hustled on to the set, and by the time the camera cut back to Maddy she was saying quite calmly, 'Well, Comfort has had to leave us, but here is Lars Jansen, who has just arrived in London...'

And she carried on so smoothly that no one realised there had ever been a hitch.

Morgan Evans was delighted with her. 'I've never seen anything smoother. Why, you might have been doing it for years.' And Maddy really began to feel that she had.

By now she knew all the camera crews, and the commissionaires, and the make-up girls, and each week when she walked into the studio she felt very at home.

The editorial board of *The World of Youth* still frequented the studio very regularly, and Mr Stanley, having saved her from suspension, was inclined to regard Maddy as his special protégée. They were all very pleased with the way the circulation of their magazine had increased since the television series had started, and asked Maddy if she would write an article entitled 'My Week' for the magazine. The article was to be in diary form, telling exactly what Maddy did every day of the week while rehearsing and transmitting the show.

Maddy took a great deal of trouble with the first article, and when finished she was rather pleased with it. Mr Stanley, however, was horrified at some passages.

'You just *cannot* say "Miss Tibbs writes the scripts, and then Mr Morgan Evans alters it all."'

'But it's true,' argued Maddy.

'That's no reason for saying it,' began Mr Stanley, then added, 'so bluntly.'

This passage was altered to 'Miss Tibbs writes the script and Mr Morgan Evans makes any alterations that are necessary.'

In fact, the whole article was edited so severely that when it appeared in the magazine Maddy hardly recognised it. But they published a big photograph of her, and several small ones taken in the studio, and sent her a cheque for a few guineas, so she didn't really mind.

Maddy had written home to her mother and father telling them with great excitement about the trip to Paris, and asking if her mother would like to go too. Mrs Fayne had replied that, while she was delighted at Maddy's good fortune, she did not feel that she could travel so far from Mr Fayne, who had not been well. If Maddy was happy to go with her usual chaperone her parents had no objection. But, her mother went on, she would come up to London to help Maddy get ready for the Paris trip and to buy her some new clothes.

The salary that Maddy was earning for the show was piling up nicely in the bank at Fenchester for, as she was too young to have a banking account, all the cheques were sent to her father. She was growing out of all her clothes so fast that it was imperative that she have some new ones.

When she mentioned this to Morgan Evans he said, 'That's a good idea. The programme will pay you back for anything you buy to wear in the show. I'm glad your mother's coming up. I don't really trust your taste—nor Sunny's, nor my own—nor Miss Tibbs's, come to that. I had been thinking of sending you out shopping with my secretary.'

Maddy, too, was glad that her mother was coming up to town, for she was longing to show her all round the studios, and to have her watch her in action during a transmission. She wrote to ask her mother whether she should book a room at an hotel for her, but Mrs Fayne replied that she would rather stay at 'The Boshery', so that she could be with Maddy all the time.

Mrs Bosham was extremely flattered at this, but was rather worried, because she had not got a room to offer Mrs Fayne.

'It doesn't matter,' said Maddy. 'She can sleep in Zillah's bed.'

'Oh, I do wish I could get some new curtains for your room.'

'I should just clean the windows,' Maddy suggested, not without good reason.

Maddy obtained permission for her mother to come and watch a Saturday transmission. She booked seats for a theatre, after asking at the ticket agency if the play was 'suitable for mothers', and she asked Sunny to come and have lunch with them one day during her mother's stay.

'I sure will, thank you, Miss Maddy,' said Sunny.

On the Thursday on which her mother was arriving, Maddy was up bright and early to tidy her room, and help Mrs Bosham make up the other bed. Then she put on her best blue, which was well above her knees by now, and wrestled with her hair, and even cleaned her shoes.

She was at Paddington long before the train arrived, and in order to pass the time went round using up her odd coppers in trying out the slot machines. She got some chewing gum, some cigarettes for her mother, then remembered that she didn't smoke, some cough sweets, and was just thinking of experimenting with a machine that sold soft drinks in cardboard cartons when the train steamed in.

Everybody in the world except her mother seemed to be getting off the train, but then she saw her, looking strangely smart in Londonish clothes.

'Mummy!' shrieked Maddy, and jumped up and down and waved.

As they hugged each other Maddy realised how much she had missed her.

II

MRS FAYNE

'Don't you look smart!' cried Maddy, almost accusingly.

'Don't you look tall!' replied her mother, holding her at arm's length to get a better view. 'Why, you're not really plump any more!'

Maddy looked down at herself in surprise.

'No, I suppose I'm not. How's Daddy? And Sandra?'

As Mrs Fayne had a suitcase they took a taxi to Fitzherbert Street. Mrs Fayne had heard a lot about 'The Boshery' from all the Blue Door Theatre Company, but she had never been there before, and was somewhat surprised at finding such a shabby street, and a little startled at Mrs Bosham, who immediately offered her a 'nice cuppa'.

'No, thank you very much,' said Maddy. 'I'm taking Mummy out to tea.' And she added afterwards to her mother, 'You see, she doesn't really "do" teas.'

'She seems very kind,' said Mrs Fayne doubtfully.

Maddy took her mother to Raddler's. It now seemed strangely empty and quiet, with all the students departed. They had tea on the first floor, where parents were always taken, and Mrs Fayne was very much interested to see the places that she had heard so much about from her children.

'We'll walk round and have a look at the Academy, if you like,' said Maddy. 'It's a pity you couldn't have come to see the end-of-term shows.'

Maddy showed her the outside of the Academy building with pride, and the schoolhouse with a little less enthusiasm.

'You know, Maddy, now that I'm here and see all the traffic and everything, I begin to think that I've been mad to let you wander about London by yourself. It was all right while the others were here, but...'

'Oh, don't worry, Mummy,' said Maddy hastily. 'I'm hardly ever by myself. Most of the time there's Zillah. She's much older than me, you know. And then there's Sunny—she's quite old. Almost as old as you. She's over thirty.'

'I'm looking forward to meeting her,' said Mrs Fayne. 'She's very good in the programme. We have enormous parties in every Saturday to watch it, you know. Sometimes the Blue Doors rush back between their matinee and evening show to see it.'

'Do they really?' said Maddy, highly flattered.

'And they keep saying you'll be too important to come back and join them when you leave the Academy.'

'Of course I shan't,' cried Maddy. 'I can't wait to be old enough to come back and be a Blue Door again. Why, I don't even want to do the Senior Course. I want to come back as soon as I reach school-leaving age. Can I, Mummy?'

'Oh dear, I really don't know what to say,' said her mother in a quandary. 'Of course I want you home as soon as possible, but I think Daddy will expect you to do the Senior Course as Sandra did.'

'But Sandra didn't do the Junior Course,' argued Maddy.

'Well, we shall just have to see what happens,' said her mother. 'You seem to do such surprising things, that it's not really worth planning for you.'

'But you are glad about me doing this television, aren't you?' Maddy pressed her.

'Of course, dear,' said her mother hastily. 'We're very proud of you indeed.'

That night Mrs Bosham made a real effort over the dinner, which Maddy and her mother had by themselves before the other lodgers came in. The soup had so much seasoning in that after the last mouthfuls they were gasping as they swallowed glasses of water. The potatoes were mashed into a series of corrugated lumps, and the steak was done to a frazzle.

'Is it always like this?' Mrs Fayne whispered, surveying the watery cabbage.

'Worse, usually,' said Maddy cheerfully.

'Oh dear, oh dear! And to think I never believed you when you said the food was bad. I thought you were just being faddy.'

'Still, it's cheap,' said Maddy. 'Do you know, I'm in the cheapest digs of anyone in the Academy.'

'I should think so too.'

But when Mrs Bosham came in, beaming all over her plump face to ask, 'Was it all right?' Mrs Fayne could not help saying brightly, 'Oh, yes. We're enjoying ourselves, Mrs Bosham.'

Their lunch next day was a very different matter. Mrs Fayne met Maddy and Sunny, and they went by taxi to a small and exclusive restaurant in Jermyn Street. Maddy and Sunny exclaimed with delight at the pink-shaded lights and the long upholstered seats round the walls.

Mrs Fayne was captivated by Sunny from the start, and had no qualms about the forthcoming trip to Paris.

After lunch Sunny left them, and they went in search of new clothes for Maddy. It was lovely to spend money, and to know that it was going to be refunded. They bought a sprigged cotton dress with a very full skirt, a loose blazer jacket, some white sandals and a Swiss cardigan, lavishly embroidered in bright colours.

'I hope nothing's too white for the cameras,' Maddy kept worrying.

'There now,' said Mrs Fayne, when they were quite exhausted. 'I think you're well set up. Let's have tea.'

'Shopping does make me hungry,' remarked Maddy as they went into Fuller's.

'You'd better have a good feast now if we're to face another Boshery meal before we go to the theatre,' said Mrs Fayne.

Maddy took her at her word, and when she had finished could not bear the thought of another meal. Fortunately, on reaching Fitzherbert Street they found that Mrs Bosham had provided cold meat and salad, which they were able to leave until they came home from the theatre.

The play proved to be extremely 'suitable for mothers'; in fact they both enjoyed it very much, and realised that it was the first time they had ever been to a West End theatre together.

'Do you want to come to the studios for the whole day tomorrow, or just for the afternoon?' asked Maddy over supper.

'I'd love to come for the whole day, but as there's some shopping I must do for myself, I think I'd better come just in the afternoon.'

Next morning Mrs Fayne was very much surprised to see Maddy leap out of bed without being called, hurry to the bathroom, return with a shiny, well-scrubbed look, and then dress herself carefully and do her hair neatly.

'This *is* a change,' she remarked as she drank the strong black tea that Mrs Bosham had brought her.

'Well,' said Maddy gloomily, 'you never know who's going to see you—all those millions of people. I must fly now; see you this afternoon. Mind you don't walk in front of any cameras.'

Mrs Fayne promised faithfully that she would be extremely careful.

At the studio there was an air of excitement this Saturday, because of the forthcoming trip to Paris. In every spare moment Morgan Evans was giving Maddy and Sunny instructions about what they were to wear and to take with them.

By now Maddy had become so used to studio rehearsals that she was never nervous until just before transmission.

Today she kept a weather eye open for her mother, and soon after they had started in the afternoon she saw Mrs Fayne in the gallery that went round the studio, and where visitors were sometimes allowed to sit. Maddy waved to her, and in doing so missed the cue that the floor manager was giving her. Over the loudspeaker Morgan Evans spoke in a voice of thunder.

'Maddy! Concentrate! I *saw* you waving to someone.'

'I'm sorry. It was my mother,' said Maddy.

'Oh—well, somebody bring her up to the control room.'

The call-boy was dispatched to fetch Mrs Fayne, and the rehearsal continued.

When they broke for tea Mrs Fayne seemed amazed at all she had seen.

'I didn't imagine it would be like this,' she said. 'I thought it would be more—well—more *furnished*! Not a great barn of a place, with all this *stuff* in the middle.'

By 'stuff' she meant the equipment and cameras that were milling about in the centre of the studio floor.

'Mr Morgan Evans is charming,' said Mrs Fayne as they went to have tea. 'And he seems to have such a high opinion of you.'

'*Does* he?' said Maddy in surprise. 'I should never have thought so.'

'Oh, yes, he spoke very highly of you. He says he's sorry this series is nearly over, and hopes to work with you again.'

'Well!' said Maddy. 'You do surprise me!'

'He did mention some trouble or other which had blown over—but he seems to think I would have heard all about it. And he said he saw that it was as much his fault as yours. Have you been up to something you haven't told me about?'

'Oh, not really,' said Maddy airily. 'It was just a little— misunderstanding. Mind the cable...'

She saved her mother from tripping over a camera cable and changed the conversation.

'Are you enjoying the show? Do you think it's good this week?'

'With so much going on, it's hard to tell,' said Mrs Fayne. 'I never realised it was as difficult as this—I thought you sat in front of a camera and it all happened.'

'Just you watch the transmission in the viewing room,' Maddy told her, 'and the whole thing will look easy again—I hope.'

Before the transmission started the floor manager shouted, 'The producer says will those going on the Paris trip stay behind for a last-minute briefing.'

There were groans of envy from the stay-at-homes.

Maddy tried to be extra good because her mother was watching in the viewing room, but the programme went much as usual. That is, the bits that had seemed difficult on rehearsal went perfectly well, and quite unforeseen problems arose in their place.

When it was over Morgan Evans came down, saying as usual, 'Jolly good show, everyone,' and then said, 'Maddy and Sunny, stay behind, won't you? Where is your mother, Maddy?'

'In the viewing room.'

'Call-boy, fetch Mrs Fayne from the viewing room, will you, and bring her here—she ought to be in on this.'

They sat in a row on chairs in the middle of the studio, while the scenery was taken down all around them, and Morgan Evans said, 'Well, Monday morning is zero hour. I want you to be at Waterloo at six o'clock. Mrs Fayne, will you see that Maddy makes it in time?'

'I'll do my best,' said Mrs Fayne. 'And then I'll hand her over to Miss Mackenzie's tender care.'

There were a lot of details about passports and so on to be settled, and Morgan Evans's secretary was scurrying about like a beaver, trying to get it all sorted out. At last everything was arranged, though Maddy was still wondering what exactly it was she had to *do* in Paris.

When the other people had departed Morgan Evans turned to Mrs Fayne and said, 'Will you and Maddy do me the honour of dining with me?'

'We should love to, shouldn't we?' Mrs Fayne turned to Maddy.

'Gosh, yes. Anything's better than a meal at the Boshery. No, no, I didn't mean it like that...'

'I shouldn't try to improve on it,' laughed Morgan Evans.

'We'd like to go home first and freshen up,' said Mrs Fayne. 'It's amazing how dirty one gets in London.'

'Well, suppose you go home now and I'll pick you up about seven-thirty.'

Maddy and Mrs Fayne hurried back to 37 Fitzherbert Street and washed and changed. They told Mrs Bosham that they would, unfortunately, have to go out, and she replied, 'There now, and I'd made you a lovely 'ash.'

'Lucky escape,' whispered Maddy to her mother when Mrs Bosham was out of hearing. ''Er 'ash is 'orrid.'

Morgan Evans arrived punctually in a taxi and took them to a Soho restaurant only a few streets away. During dinner he told them all about his boyhood in a mining village in South Wales, and they both listened spellbound, though Maddy did not forget to eat at the same time.

When she finished the last drop of her fruit salad she said, 'It's nice when you come up to town, Mummy. I've had more good meals since you came than I've had in all the rest of term put together.'

'You *do* say charming things, Maddy,' laughed her mother. 'But I'm glad you haven't lost your interest in food.'

'Wait till we get to Paris, if you want good food,' Morgan Evans told her. 'But mind you don't eat so much that you're not in a fit state to work.'

'What exactly have I got to *do* in Paris?' Maddy wanted to know. 'I don't quite understand about the filming.'

'Well, we've arranged with a French family that you and Sunny shall stay with them, and they will take you round Paris and show you the sights, and we shall have a film cameraman recording it. There won't be any sound on the film; it will be silent, because it's so much simpler, and when the film is shown next Saturday—isn't that an awful thought!—you will have to speak the commentary. Now do you understand better?'

'Ye-es,' said Maddy. 'There's just one drawback. I don't speak French and neither does Sunny.'

'That doesn't matter,' said Morgan Evans. 'We've chosen the family very carefully, and the children speak quite good English.'

'Oh, thank heavens,' said Maddy. 'I couldn't bear having to talk about the pen of my aunt, and the gardener's penknife all the time.'

When they had finished their coffee Mrs Fayne noticed how tired Maddy looked. 'I must tuck you up early tonight, Maddy,' she said.

'Yes, and see that she has a really good rest tomorrow,' added Morgan Evans. 'Next week is going to be extremely hectic, and I don't want to knock her out in the last week of the series. She's stood up to it very well until now.'

'Yes.' agreed Mrs Fayne. 'And when the excitement of next week is over she's coming back to Fenchester, and will be able to have a good rest before term starts.'

'Oh, can't I do some shows at the Blue Door Theatre?' cried Maddy. 'I thought there might just be time...'

'No!' said her mother very firmly. 'You're going to have a real rest. And haven't you any holiday tasks to do?'

'Er—yes—I believe I have,' said Maddy vaguely.

'Then you'll have a chance to get on with them.'

'I thought you said I was to have a real rest?'

'I meant physically.'

Maddy was so sleepy after the long transmission day and then the enormous meal, that she was nearly asleep on her feet, and Morgan Evans insisted on hailing a taxi outside the restaurant to take them the short distance to Fitzherbert Street.

'It's been a delightful evening,' said Mrs Fayne sincerely as they arrived at number thirty-seven. 'And I must say that I have no qualms at all about Maddy going to Paris, now that I have seen the people she is going with.'

The next morning Mrs Fayne made Maddy stay in bed for breakfast. In fact they both had breakfast in bed, as Mrs Bosham appeared with trays before Mrs Fayne was fully dressed, so she went back to bed and revelled in the doubtful luxury of underdone eggs and overdone toast that she had not had to prepare herself.

She managed to keep Maddy in bed until about eleven, but then the sun was shining so brightly that Maddy leapt out of bed saying, 'I can't stay here another minute. Let's go for a walk in Regent's Park.'

She showed her mother all the favourite spots where she and Zillah learnt their parts, and then they came back to 'The Boshery' for an indigestible Sunday lunch with the other lodgers.

When the meal was over they were so full of soggy Yorkshire pudding that they went and lay down. Maddy intended to read, but fell asleep, and did not wake until Mrs Bosham brought up cups of tea at four o'clock.

'Now this evening I really must do your packing for you, Maddy,' said Mrs Fayne, 'so that you're all ready to start off early tomorrow.'

Maddy was secretly a little amused that her mother should take it for granted that her packing must be done for her. By this time Maddy was so used to packing up her things for transmission day, and for shows at the Academy, that preparation for a trip to Paris seemed hardly more serious. However, it was nice to have someone to do the necessary repairs that became apparent as the packing proceeded.

'Maddy! How long have you had a safety pin in here?' demanded her mother, holding up her dressing-gown.

'Weeks,' said Maddy calmly.

'Oh dear, oh dear, and all your shoes need heeling!'

'I'll only take my new white sandals,' said Maddy.

'Don't be silly, dear. Suppose it rains?'

Mrs Fayne had bought Maddy a suitcase. It was a special lightweight one for air travel, and was grey with a few red stripes. Maddy thought it was the smartest she had ever seen.

At last it was neatly packed with all her new clothes, and her faithful blue dress 'just in case'. She was to travel in her grey skirt and the new red blazer.

'And my suitcase is all to match,' Maddy said, delighted.

Somehow, although they had intended to have an early night, it developed into quite a late one, for Mrs Fayne kept on discovering last-minute things to be done.

They found that Maddy's brush and comb had been left out, and after an inspection Mrs Fayne decided that they must be washed. Then she remembered that she must do her own packing, as she did not want to have to come back to Fitzherbert Street after seeing Maddy off.

At last they were ready to go to bed, but Maddy could not get to sleep for excitement. She had never been in an aeroplane. Neither had she been abroad before. The prospect of doing both the very next day made sleep impossible.

She was in the throes of thinking that she could never get to sleep before morning, when suddenly it was daylight and the alarm clock was ringing.

At first she was so sleepy that she felt that she could not be bothered to go to Paris that day—but suddenly she leapt out of bed, nearly tripping over her new suitcase.

'Mummy, it's today,' she cried, and then raced into the bathroom, remembering half-way to try and be quiet and not disturb the other lodgers.

Mrs Bosham had insisted on getting up to give them their breakfast, and was slopping about in bedroom slippers and an incredible dressing-gown with her hair in metal curlers.

It was all a mad rush, because they had to be at Waterloo at six. The street still had a very early-morning look as they climbed into the hire-car that had been sent by the studios.

'Goodbye! Good Luck! Or should I say, "Bong voyagey",'

cried Mrs Bosham from the front doorstep, waving one of the milk bottles that she had picked up.

'Now, do be good, Maddy,' her mother urged her as they drove through empty streets. 'Do just as you're told, and don't wander away from the others. And don't eat too much rich food. And don't drink wine, even if you see the French children doing so. You can't afford to have an upset stomach when you're going to be so busy.'

'Yes, Mummy. No, Mummy,' said Maddy dutifully all the way to Waterloo.

When they got there they were met by Morgan Evans, his secretary, Guy his assistant, a film cameraman and *his* assistant, and Miss Tibbs, all looking rather pale and early morning-ish, and Sunny—looking as cheerful as ever.

By this time Maddy was so excited that she could hardly keep still. There were a few formalities to go through, and then they had to pile into the bus that would take them to the airport. Mrs Fayne was not coming to the airport as she was anxious to get back to Fenchester in good time.

'Goodbye, dear, and *do* be good,' she begged. 'And come back to Fenchester as soon as you can next week, won't you? And send me a card the minute you arrive in Paris.'

'Goodbye, Mummy,' said Maddy, as she kissed her.

'Thanks for coming to get me off. Give my love to Daddy and tell the others I'll see them soon.'

Somehow, London looked very different and quite exciting from the window of the airline bus. Maddy sat beside Morgan Evans, and chattered sixteen to the dozen.

'Really, Maddy,' he said rather weakly, 'I don't know how you can...'

'Can what?'

'Talk at such a rate at this hour.'

'I'm sorry. I'm just excited.'

When they got to the airport it was even more exciting—for there were the beautiful silver planes lined up on the tarmac.

'Are we going in one of those?' demanded Maddy. 'Which one do you think?'

There were long delays while their passports were checked and they went through the Customs. But Maddy was thrilled with the enormous clean airy halls and the smart air hostesses hurrying about in beautifully tailored uniforms.

When she was asked if she had anything of value in her suitcase Maddy replied, 'Yes, I've got a new sprigged cotton dress, and a Swiss cardigan, and...'

'No watches, cameras, typewriters, jewellery?'

'Only my string of corals that Sandra gave me.'

The official smiled kindly and made a chalk squiggle over her brand-new suitcase. Maddy promptly licked her finger and rubbed it off again.

'Hey, you mustn't do that,' the official told her. 'That's to show it's been checked.'

'Well, do you mind doing a very small one. You see, it's new,' said Maddy.

Obediently he made a very faint scribble on it.

They had to spend a long time waiting in the lounge, where they drank cups of tea and Maddy surprised everyone by eating two doughnuts. Even Sunny felt bound to say, 'Now, honey, remember you're going in an aeroplane.'

'I'll be all right,' said Maddy. 'These will stop that sinking feeling.'

It seemed ridiculous to have to get up so early in the morning and then wait for so long. The cameraman, whose name was Bill, and his assistant, an elderly man called Charles, both had 'forty winks', and Miss Tibbs started making notes for her script.

'We don't want any shots of you getting into the plane.' Morgan Evans told Maddy, 'because, if you remember, in the script you're not supposed to be coming from England—you're on your way there. But I want a shot of you and Sunny getting off the plane at Orly Airport. So remember to tidy up before we actually arrive.'

At last the loudspeaker blared out that their flight was ready, and they all trooped along behind an air hostess, who led them out to a bus which took them some distance to the waiting plane.

'Oh, isn't it a lovely little thing!' breathed Maddy.

And it did look quite small because of the neatness of its design. Maddy walked up the gangway feeling so excited that she felt she might take off on her own accord before the plane did. She shared a seat with Sunny this time, saying, 'I think I was a little too much for Mr Evans in the bus.'

The air hostess came round, showing them how to fasten their safety belts before the take-off.

'Will it be bumpy?' asked Maddy hopefully.

'It shouldn't be,' said the hostess. 'The weather report is good, so it should be pretty smooth. But have some barley sugar if you're doubtful.'

Maddy accepted the barley sugar gratefully.

'That'll settle the doughnuts,' she told Sunny.

She and Sunny were the only passengers who had not flown before, so they compared symptoms.

'My inside is feeling funny already,' complained Sunny. 'So please don't talk to me about doughnuts and barley sugar...'

'That's just imagination,' Maddy told her.

When the engines started up and the plane vibrated Maddy thought that they were about to take off, and sat forward in her seat to look out of the window, as she did not want to miss a moment of her first flight.

'We're off, we're off!' she shouted to Sunny as the plane taxied into position. Then suddenly the roar of the engines seemed to stop.

'Oh, Miss Maddy, Miss Maddy,' gasped Sunny. 'It's gone wrong, it's gone wrong!'

'Don't worry,' said Morgan Evans, leaning over to her, 'that was only to warm up the engines. We'll be off in a minute.'

It was difficult to tell the exact moment when the plane became airborne, for when its engines roared again it taxied a long way before, suddenly, Maddy could see that there was some distance between the plane and the earth.

'We're off!' she shouted again so loudly that the other passengers smiled. Fascinated, she watched the earth fade farther and farther away, until the houses and buildings looked like toys. And then they were up among the cotton-wool clouds that came so close to the plane that Maddy longed to lean out and touch them.

Surprisingly soon, the novelty faded, and when breakfast trays were brought round Maddy was able to devote all her attention to the meal. Nobody else in their party had more than coffee and rolls, and Morgan Evans said warningly,

'Maddy, *do* be careful. You'll probably be expected to eat quite large meals in Paris.'

'Flying makes me hungry,' said Maddy as she finished her fruit juice and cereal, and proceeded to attack the deliciously crisp fresh rolls and marmalade that the hostess had just brought round.

It was an amazingly short journey. While breakfast was being served they crossed the Channel, seeing the blue stretch of sea below; and scarcely was breakfast over than they were again instructed to fasten their safety belts, and there, stretched out all silver and grey in the morning mist, was Paris.

Maddy and Sunny tidied their hair frantically, and Sunny powdered her face. Maddy begged to be allowed some powder as her face was all shiny with excitement, but Morgan Evans said sharply, 'Certainly not, Maddy. We'd never match you up in the studio if you had any make-up on now.'

Bill and Charles were busy getting the camera ready to take shots of the arrival, but Maddy was too thrilled at the thought of being in a foreign country to think of filming.

She walked reverently down the gangway thinking, 'At last I set foot on foreign soil,' but was rudely awakened by Morgan Evans saying, 'Yes, do you mind going back again— Maddy and Sunny. We'll get lined up on the shots then give you the cue.'

12

CHEZ LEFÈVRE

Maddy found it was the same all the way through the trip. Whenever she had just done something important for the first time she had to go back and do it again for the film camera to take, which made everything seem rather an anticlimax.

After they had taken shots of Maddy and Sunny descending the gangway, they had to go into the airport building and go through the passport checking and the Customs again.

'*Rien à déclarer?*' shouted a fierce little man with an equally fierce moustache, right in Maddy's face.

'Eh, what?' she spluttered.

'*Rien!*' Morgan Evans replied for her with great energy.

'Oh, I see,' said Maddy. 'Anything to declare.'

It was all so bewildering, because everybody talked so fast and waved their arms about so much. Instead of the orderly queue that there had been for the Customs when they left England, everyone was pushing and jostling, and doing their best to get attention before everyone else.

'Now, when we get into Paris.' Morgan Evans told them, 'Maddy and Sunny and I will go by taxi to the Lefèvres'. Everyone else will go to the hotel, dump their baggage, get some lunch, and then come over to the Lefèvres'. Guy's got the address. Now don't for heaven's sake get lost, or we shall waste the whole afternoon.'

Going into Paris from Orly in the airport bus Maddy was terribly excited to see all the advertisements printed in French.

'What does that mean? What does that mean?' she kept clamouring, and her triumph knew no bounds when she recognised a word or a phrase.

When they got off the bus at the air terminal they stood in an untidy group trying to hail a taxi. The traffic swooped round them.

'All on the wrong side of the road,' said Maddy.

Morgan Evans found a taxi at last and bundled Maddy and Sunny into it. He gave the Lefèvres' address to the driver, who protested that he had never heard of it until he saw it written down, and then drove off at a fantastic speed. Maddy and Sunny clung together squealing, as the taxi raced round corners on two wheels and the driver leaned out of the window to shout at other drivers.

It seemed a very long ride to the suburb where the Lefèvres lived and Sunny kept worrying about the way the meter was ticking up.

'Don't worry,' Morgan Evans told her. 'The firm's paying.'

At last the streets of shops and cafés gave place to rows of houses with gardens in front, and eventually the cab stopped in front of a neat-looking house behind a high hedge.

At the windows it had shutters painted a cheerful pink.

'What a lovely little house,' cried Maddy. 'Is this where we're going to stay?'

'Yes,' Morgan Evans told her. 'Hop out. We're late already.'

The front door opened and out came a man and woman with a girl and a boy in their teens. They advanced with welcoming smiles, and all shook hands with Morgan Evans, who talked to them in French, and then introduced Maddy and Sunny. Instantly the family switched from speaking French to speaking English, and the girl and boy shook hands and greeted them.

The mother, who was very small and neat, with dark hair and shining eyes, urged them to come inside, as lunch was ready.

Morgan Evans passed over a number of grubby notes to the driver, and asked him to return at three o'clock to take them into Paris again.

Inside the house, which was light and airy and neat as a new pin, Madame Lefèvre showed Maddy and Sunny to their rooms, which were obviously the best, and had modern handbasins.

Maddy washed, changed into her new print dress and went downstairs, where the most delicious meal was awaiting them in the dining-room. First came soup in an enormous tureen. This was so delicious that Maddy had two helpings, then regretted it when she realised how much more there was to follow. Next were tiny fish cooked in batter as a course by themselves, then succulent steak with very thin chips, and, as another separate course, green beans with butter on top. By this time Maddy had surreptitiously loosened her belt and hoped that no one had noticed.

She could not do justice to the selection of cheeses and fruit that followed, but just nibbled at them and, almost for the first time, took stock of the Lefèvre girl and boy.

Jacqueline was very like her mother, only rather thin, and Pierre looked grown-up for fifteen. The father was large and jovial and laughed a lot, and patted people on the shoulder and slapped them on the back.

Sunny was a great success. They loved her American accent and her fruity laugh.

Before they knew where they were there was a ringing at the door, and the rest of the unit had arrived, and it was time to start filming.

'First of all,' said Morgan Evans, 'I want Maddy and Sunny getting out of the taxi, and being greeted by Pierre and Jacqueline.'

And so they had to enact the whole arrival again, with the camera whirring and it needed four 'takes' before it was correct.

Then they took some shots of the house and Maddy and Sunny being shown round, featuring the dovecot in the back garden where the Lefèvres kept pet doves.

About half past four, when the other taxi had arrived and had been waiting over an hour, they were able to set off for some sightseeing in the centre of Paris. The unit filled two taxis, and the Lefèvres followed in their ancient little Citroen.

By this time Maddy was quite sleepy after such an early start and enormous lunch. Morgan Evans, seeing her drowsing in the corner of the taxi said, 'Wake up, Maddy. We've only just started work. We'll have to get a move on before the light goes. Thank heavens the evenings are pretty long.'

The excitement of seeing the Arc de Triomphe at the end of the long avenue of the Champs-Élysées roused her a bit, and they all tumbled out of the taxis to get shots of Maddy and Sunny being shown it by Pierre and Jacqueline.

'It's just like our Marble Arch,' said Maddy, surprised.

'Yes,' agreed Morgan Evans, 'but shown off to better advantage.'

Quite a crowd gathered to watch the filming, and Guy and the secretary, and even Miss Tibbs, were kept busy trying to keep passers-by from walking in front of the cameras. Miss Tibbs gabbled away at them in very good French, waving the shooting stick that she had brought with her.

Maddy soon wished that she too had brought a shooting stick, for her legs ached with standing about between shots. Morgan Evans was frantically trying to hurry everyone up, but the cameraman and his assistant could not be hurried. Every shot had to be just right, and they checked and rechecked the amount of light and the distance of the people from the camera.

At last they moved on to the gardens of the Bois de Boulogne, where they all had glasses of lemonade, and took shots of Maddy, Sunny and the Lefèvre children drinking. Then they drove to the Louvre, and took shots of them walking up the steps.

'Can't we go in and look round?' asked Maddy. 'I want to see that Venus with no arms. She is here, isn't she?'

'Yes, yes,' said Jacqueline proudly, almost as though she had put her there herself.

'No, I'm sorry,' said Morgan Evans firmly. 'There just isn't time. We've got so much to get through, and only the rest of today and tomorrow to do it in. Now we must get down to the Quais...'

Maddy was enthralled by the Seine. She could have stood by the parapet and looked down at the water, with the barges and the motorboats going by, for the rest of the evening, but they could only take a few shots before it was time to hurry off to the cathedral of Notre-Dame. Here Maddy remembered that she had not sent a postcard to her mother, so she bought one for her and one for Zillah, and wrote them while they were lining up the shots.

'I'm here. It's wonderful. I'm seeing absolutely everything, and eating loads. Love to all, Maddy.'

While they were packing up the equipment, Maddy and Sunny managed to slip inside the cathedral, and tiptoed round in awe, trying not to disturb an evening service that was in progress.

It was so soothing and so dim after the bright sunlight outside that it seemed like a different world.

When they came out Morgan Evans was champing at the bit to be off.

'Quick,' he urged them. 'The light's going—the light's going.'

'Where are we off to now?' asked Maddy. 'The Eiffel Tower? We haven't been there yet.'

'No—we're doing the Eiffel Tower tomorrow,' he told them. 'But we must get shots of the Sacré-Coeur before we finish.'

'What's the Sacré-Coeur?' demanded Maddy, as they tumbled into the taxis.

'It is a—basilique,' said Jacqueline. 'I do not know how else to call it.'

'It's a church with a dome on top—we call it a basilica—right on top of Montmartre,' explained Morgan Evans.

They had to leave the cars at the bottom of one of the steep hills up to Montmartre, and climb up steep flights of steps, with a handrail to cling to, in order to reach the church of the Sacred Heart. The sun was beginning to set, throwing pink rays on to the gleaming white dome.

They toiled up the steps, stopping every few minutes to admire the building in front of them. The Lefèvre family seemed as proud of it as they had been of all the other famous places in their city. Exhausted, the visitors leaned on the railings at the top of the steps and looked out over Paris, while the cameramen unpacked the equipment once more.

'Oh, I've sure got "Paris Foot",' moaned Sunny, slipping off one high-heeled shoe after the other. 'Mr Evans, do you mind a barefooted Southern gal in these shots?'

'This is the last lap, everyone,' Morgan Evans urged them on. 'The sun will only last a few more minutes. Ready, Bill?'

The cameramen had stopped on the terrace below the uppermost one, and were setting up the camera ready to take a shot of Maddy and Sunny walking up the last flight of steps.

'Oh, gee, I can't,' moaned Sunny, but she did.

Happily they got this shot in one take, and then were able to have a short rest while they took shots of the church from several angles.

'Quickly, quickly,' urged Morgan Evans. 'The sun's nearly gone. Can you manage one more, Bill?'

'Well, it's pretty bad,' said the cameraman gloomily, 'but we'll have a go.'

'The four of them going in through the door—I know of some stock shots of the interior that we can hire from a film library in London.'

They managed to get a last shot before the sun went.

'Right,' cried Morgan Evans with satisfaction. 'We can break now. Thank you, everyone. Do what you like for the rest of the evening, but don't be too late—however tempting it is. I want to start at seven-thirty tomorrow morning.'

Nobody had the energy to do anything but flop on to a seat on the steep grassy slopes, and ease their shoes off.

'I should like to put my feet into a bath of ice-cream,' said Maddy dreamily.

'You would like to bath yourself?' inquired Madame Lefèvre anxiously. 'You wish to return to the home—and rest?'

'Oh, no, no,' cried Maddy, 'not really. I was just joking. I don't want to miss a moment of this glorious evening. Paris must be the most beautiful place in the world.'

After they had sat there for a time they all felt thirsty, and so they descended the steep steps to a little café at the foot, and sat outside on the pavement under stripey awnings and drank their own particular favourite liquids. The Englishmen of the party drank beer, the entire Lefèvre family drank wine; Maddy remembered what her mother had said, and she and Sunny had lemonade made of real lemons squeezed at the table. The secretary and Miss Tibbs had crème-de-menthe, which made them even thirstier, and they washed it down with vast quantities of water. The camera crew, the secretary, Guy and Miss Tibbs then went back to the hotel to change and have dinner, but Morgan Evans remained with Maddy and Sunny and the Lefèvres.

'I should be most pleased if you would dine with us, Monsieur Evans,' said Monsieur Lefèvre.

'On the contrary,' said Morgan Evans, 'you and your family must dine with *us*.'

'How can they?' asked Maddy. 'We don't live here.'

'At a restaurant, of course,' said Morgan Evans. 'Perhaps you could recommend somewhere, Monsieur.'

'Yes, indeed. There is a most amusing one behind the basilique,' said Monsieur Lefèvre. 'The little ones would enjoy themselves well. But it is not cheap.'

'It's all on the firm,' said Morgan Evans. 'We are so grateful to you for co-operating with us like this.'

'I wish,' said Jacqueline wistfully, 'that it was possible I might see these films, when they are finished.'

'Yes, it's a pity that you cannot see our television. But we will send you some stills—some photographs from them,' promised Morgan Evans.

'You are rested?' asked Monsieur Lefèvre. 'Then it is necessary to mount the steps again. I am so sorry.'

By this time it was cooler and becoming dusk, and the climb did not seem so much of a hardship.

Behind the Sacré-Coeur was a mass of little streets, full of restaurants and bars and cafés, bookshops, picture shops, handicraft shops—all still open, with lights and music blaring out. Crowds of tourists and Parisians thronged the narrow streets, and cars crawled at snail pace over the cobbles. Maddy walked as though in a dream. This was what she had always imagined Paris to be like.

The restaurant to which Monsieur Lefèvre led them was decorated to look like a gypsies' hideout, and there were female gypsies serving the food, and male gypsies playing violins. They came close up to the table and played 'right bang in your ear', as Maddy put it.

Maddy and Sunny had used so much energy since lunch time that now they were ravenous again, and ate enormously despite the violins. On the rough wood tables candles stuck in bottles threw mysterious shadows over everybody's face.

'Don't we all look much nicer by candlelight?' Maddy observed.

Towards the end of the meal she began to look back over the day and came to the conclusion that it had been the longest she had ever lived through. The plane flight of the morning seemed weeks ago.

Madame Lefèvre noticed Maddy nodding, and tried to hurry the other grown-ups over the liqueurs they were drinking with their coffee.

There was still one more journey down the steep steps to the road where the Lefèvres' car was parked. By this time the Sacré-Coeur was floodlit, and looking more than ever like something out of the Arabian Nights. When they reached the car Morgan Evans said goodnight, and after reminding them of the rendezvous at the Eiffel Tower next morning he caught a taxi back to the hotel.

It was such a squash in the car that Maddy got terrible giggles, and then Jacqueline and Pierre taught her and Sunny some French songs with loud choruses that they sang at the tops of their voices.

'It's a pity,' said Maddy thoughtfully, just before they reached the Lefèvres' house, 'that the *World of Youth* viewers can't see the *real* things that happen—I mean the Eiffel Tower doesn't really make anyone feel any *friendlier* towards anyone else, does it? But if they could see us in this car, it would.'

This was too complicated for the Lefèvres to understand, but Sunny knew what she meant.

When they reached the house Madame Lefèvre insisted that they have baths, as there would not be time in the morning.

'And I know how you English love your baths.'

'Do we?' said Maddy, surprised. 'We don't at Mrs Bosham's.'

The bathroom, all in primrose and green, with a shower over the bath, was very different from that at 'The Boshery'.

Maddy experimented with the shower and got her hair soaking wet. She was too tired to bother about drying it before she went to bed, and Madame Lefèvre was quite perturbed to see how wet it was when she came to see if Maddy was all right.

'You will catch a rheum,' she cried, and insisted on rubbing her hair with a towel. 'So blonde,' she observed, as she did so, 'a real Angel-Saxon.'

'She's no angel,' laughed Sunny, who had also come in to say goodnight.

Maddy was asleep almost before they were out of the room.

The very next minute, or so it seemed, Jacqueline was standing by the bed in broad daylight, holding out a cup of what looked like hot water, with a little bag floating in it.

'What on earth...?' inquired Maddy sleepily.

'It is the English tea. I made it for you especially.'

'How kind,' said Maddy, astounded at the look of it. 'Is this what you drink at breakfast?'

'Oh, no. We drink *café au lait*. But you may have more tea if you like.'

'No, no,' cried Maddy hastily after tasting the liquid. 'I'll have coffee too, thank you. And I'm sure Sunny will—she's American, you know.'

Maddy got dressed quickly and threw the tea down the washbasin. The most delicious smell of coffee was pervading the house.

In the dining-room the family were sitting in front of large handleless bowls of coffee, into which they were dipping croissant rolls. There was no butter, no plates or knives.

As soon as Maddy came in Pierre and Monsieur Lefèvre rose, and bowed and held out their hands. Maddy had to shake hands all round the table, and so did Sunny when she entered.

Maddy found such good manners rather a strain at half past six in the morning.

The coffee was delicious and so were the rolls. They were so crisp and rich that Maddy soon found they did not need butter or marmalade, and after a while she plucked up courage to dip hers into the coffee too, and found it very good indeed.

They had to hurry off, in order to reach the Eiffel Tower at the correct time, and then they got caught in the early-morning traffic jam, which seemed nearly as bad as in London.

They were a little late and the rest of the party were waiting for them, Bill and his assistant with the camera all ready to start, but the Lefèvres insisted on shaking hands all round.

'Maddy,' cried Morgan Evans in dismay. 'You're wearing a different dress from the one you wore yesterday.'

'Yes,' said Maddy innocently. 'My new one's looking a bit grubby, after yesterday, so I thought I'd put on my old one.'

'But these shots are supposed to match up,' moaned Morgan Evans. 'They're all supposed to be taken on one day.'

'But we'd never have had time to get all those shots in one day,' Maddy objected.

'The viewers won't know that. They'll think they were just *taken*—just like that—while you were actually arriving at places. Now, come on, where's your other dress?'

'In my case, in the car.'

'Then change into it.'

'You mean here?'

There were not many people about yet, so Miss Tibbs, Jacqueline and Madame Lefèvre, and Sunny stood against the windows of the Citroën whilst Maddy changed inside. She emerged with her hair tousled and her buttons wrongly done up, but Morgan Evans heaved a sigh of relief.

'Have we actually got to go up it?' demanded Maddy, looking rather doubtfully at the tower which appeared to be swaying in the morning breeze.

'No,' said Morgan Evans, 'not really. We'll have a shot of you starting up the steps, then we've got some still photos of the view from the top.'

'What a pity,' said Maddy.

'I sure am glad,' declared Sunny. 'My feet haven't recovered from climbing them steps yesterday.'

After they had finished the Eiffel Tower shots they went into the smartest shopping streets, and took some shots of Jacqueline, Sunny and Maddy window gazing. Their gestures of delight at what they saw were quite sincere, and unrehearsed. Morgan Evans was adamant that there was no time for going inside shops, but they did manage to slip inside the Galeries Lafayette for a moment while Morgan Evans was busy getting a shot of Pierre, walking along fed up with shopping, reading a newspaper.

The morning seemed to rush by; there was no time for a coffee break, and it began to get hotter and hotter. The children bought ice-creams and licked at them between takes, but they melted in the hands of the kind people they were parked with when their owners were required in front of the camera.

By one o'clock they were hungry and thirsty and very tired.

'I must have some shots of the Luxembourg Gardens,' cried Morgan Evans, 'and the plane goes at five—there's no time for lunch.'

But it was impossible for them to go on without refreshment.

'Why, we had breakfast just after six,' wailed Maddy.

With the heat and the thought of no break for food tempers began to fray, and eventually Miss Tibbs and Madame

Lefèvre were dispatched to buy a picnic lunch. They returned with miniature loaves of crusty bread, butter, cheese, fruit, beer in funny little tin cans for the men, and a bottle of wine for the women, and some very strange mineral water for Maddy. They made their way to the Luxembourg Gardens by car and taxi, and there they relaxed luxuriously in the shade under a tree. At least everyone did except Bill and Charles, and they kept interrupting their lunch to take shots of people eating. But Morgan Evans was tireless; as soon as the last crumb was finished he insisted that they must press on.

'We can get some terrific shots with these pieces of statuary and the lovely long avenue to the Palace. It's a pity it's not in colour—the flowers are so wonderful.'

Before they had taken all the shots that presented themselves it was time to make for the air terminal, but there was luggage to be collected from the hotel where the unit stayed.

'We're cutting it very fine,' said Morgan Evans. 'If we miss the airway bus we'll have to race to Orly by taxi.'

They had already spent a small fortune on taxis that day. The Lefèvres came to the airport to see them off, and while they were going through the passport and Customs sheds they went out on to the airfield to look at the plane.

This time Maddy knew what 'Rien à déclarer?' meant and announced, 'Rien, pas de temps,' which rather puzzled the Customs officer.

When they said goodbye to the Lefèvres Maddy made them promise to come to Fenchester and stay with her if they ever came to England.

'Then we shall have more time to talk,' she said. 'This has all been such a rush.'

Morgan Evans thanked them formally for all the trouble they had taken, and told them that the firm would reimburse them.

'No, no, no,' objected Madame Lefèvre. 'All we should wish is to see some photos of the little ones.'

'Of course you shall,' Morgan Evans assured her. 'And now, goodbye.'

The Lefèvres stood waving, and as they boarded the plane Maddy felt quite sad at having to wave goodbye.

Bill and Charles were being very nippy, getting shots of the Lefèvres and of Maddy and Sunny, all waving.

'Come on,' called Morgan Evans at last, 'or you'll miss the plane.'

'Wish we could,' cried Bill, as they came up the gangway, which was immediately wheeled away almost from under their very feet.

'Bon voyage,' shouted the Lefèvres.

'Au revoir,' shouted Maddy.

And then the plane door was shut and it was very difficult to see out of the windows.

As soon as they had taken off, tea or coffee and cakes were served, and when these were disposed of the entire unit fell fast asleep, and did not wake until they landed.

Maddy was so tired she could scarcely keep awake to go through the Customs. Morgan Evans took her back to Fitzherbert Street in a taxi, quite alarmed that he had tired her out to such a degree.

'You're sure you'll be all right for rehearsal tomorrow?' he asked.

'Yes, of course,' said Maddy. 'I'm going straight to bed.'

She could not even be bothered to tell Mrs Bosham all her adventures, but just fell into bed and slept the clock round. She was wakened by Mrs Bosham shaking her shoulder and saying, 'Wake up, do; I've been calling you this last hour. You'll be late for rehearsal if you don't look out. Here's your breakfast—I think it's cruel to make you rehearse today. What are you going to rehearse anyway, if it was all filmed?'

Maddy couldn't tell her, for she herself didn't know. This week's rehearsal turned out to be very strange indeed. That day, which was only Wednesday, although they seemed to have been away for weeks—they merely discussed the script with Miss Tibbs. The following day they went into a tiny projection theatre, just like a miniature cinema, and saw the rushes of the film that had just been taken. They seemed very jumbly and did not make much sense. By the following day they saw the cut version, which was all pieced together properly and did make sense, and Maddy practised reading the commentary that Miss Tibbs had been busy writing.

'We're not going to dub it on the film,' said Morgan Evans. 'It will sound more natural if you do it in the studio as you watch the film on the monitor.'

To time the words perfectly to the pictures was more difficult than Maddy had imagined it would be.

Saturday arrived in a flash. It had been arranged for Sunny to be interviewed *after* the Paris film. And for some reason this interview always reduced both of them to helpless giggles.

'It's no good,' said Maddy. 'I'll never be able to ask her the usual questions without giggling. Can't we just talk?'

'Well,' said Morgan Evans cautiously, 'yes, but for goodness' sake be careful what you say.'

'You can't suspend me this time,' said Maddy wickedly, 'because it's the last one anyhow.'

'I can pull your pigtails, though,' said Morgan Evans, and did so sharply.

There was quite a feeling of disappointment in the studio that the series was finishing. Even one of the property men came up to Maddy and said, 'Pity this is coming off. It's a good little show. One of the best we've got. Still, there's a rumour it's coming back in the spring.'

Maddy's heart lifted. If the prop men had heard that, then it must be true.

'Don't do any worse than you've done up till now, and we shall be seeing more of you, Miss Fayne,' said Morgan Evans just before the transmission.

Maddy got through the commentary very well. It was lovely seeing all the shots of Paris, and occasionally she put in an aside and a giggle, when she remembered anything funny that had happened.

The musical interlude was a respite for her, and after that she had to interview a young Javanese girl who was on the staff of *The World of Youth*.

By then the worst was over, and the last few minutes were just a little chat with Sunny, in which they recalled some of the amusing things that had happened during the run of the series. At the end of it, to Maddy's surprise, Sunny kissed her warmly on both cheeks saying, 'Well, goodbye, honey, I wouldn't have missed it for all the world. And so long, all you other young 'uns,' she said to the camera.

Maddy was left to make the final announcement, and she felt quite choky as she did so. Then the transmission lights on the cameras faded, and Maddy had a strange feeling that she too was fading away.

But then she pulled herself together and remembered that all this had just been pretence—shadows on a screen—and on Monday she would be returning to home and real life, in Fenchester.

FADE SOUND AND VISION

PUSHKIN CHILDREN'S BOOKS

We created Pushkin Children's Books to share tales from different languages and cultures with younger readers, and to open the door to the wide, colourful worlds these stories offer.

From picture books and adventure stories to fairy tales and classics, and from fifty-year-old bestsellers to current huge successes abroad, the books on the Pushkin Children's list reflect the very best stories from around the world, for our most discerning readers of all: children.

THE BEGINNING WOODS

MALCOLM MCNEILL

'I loved every word and was envious of quite a few... A
modern classic. Rich, funny and terrifying'

Eoin Colfer

THE RED ABBEY CHRONICLES

MARIA TURTSCHANINOFF

1 · *Maresi*
2 · *Naondel*

'Embued with myth, wonder, and told with
a dazzling, compelling ferocity'

Kiran Millwood Hargrave, author of *The Girl of Ink and Stars*

THE LETTER FOR THE KING

TONKE DRAGT

'*The Letter for the King* will get pulses racing... Pushkin
Press deserves every praise for publishing this beautifully
translated, well-presented and captivating book'

The Times

THE SECRETS OF THE WILD WOOD

TONKE DRAGT

'Offers intrigue, action and escapism'

Sunday Times

THE SONG OF SEVEN

TONKE DRAGT

'A cracking adventure... so nail-biting you'll need to wear protective gloves'

The Times

THE MURDERER'S APE

JAKOB WEGELIUS

'A thrilling adventure. Prepare to meet the remarkable
Sally Jones; you won't soon forget her'

Publishers Weekly

THE PARENT TRAP · THE FLYING CLASSROOM · DOT AND ANTON

ERICH KÄSTNER

Illustrated by Walter Trier

'The bold line drawings by Walter Trier are the work of genius... As for the stories, if you're a fan of *Emil and the Detectives*, then you'll find these just as spirited'

Spectator

FROM THE MIXED-UP FILES OF MRS. BASIL E. FRANKWEILER

E. L. KONIGSBURG

'Delightful... I love this book... a beautifully written adventure, with endearing characters and full of dry wit, imagination and inspirational confidence'

Daily Mail

THE RECKLESS SERIES

CORNELIA FUNKE

1 · *The Petrified Flesh*
2 · *Living Shadows*
3 · *The Golden Yarn*

'A wonderful storyteller'

Sunday Times

THE WILDWITCH SERIES

LENE KAABERBØL

1 · *Wildfire*
2 · *Oblivion*
3 · *Life Stealer*
4 · *Bloodling*

'Classic fantasy adventure... Young readers will be delighted to hear that there are more adventures to come for Clara'

Lovereading

MEET AT THE ARK AT EIGHT!

ULRICH HUB

Illustrated by Jörg Mühle

'Of all the books about a penguin in a suitcase pretending to be God asking for a cheesecake, this one is absolutely, definitely my favourite'

Independent

THE SNOW QUEEN
HANS CHRISTIAN ANDERSEN

Illustrated by Lucie Arnoux

'A lovely edition [of a] timeless story'
The Lady

THE WILD SWANS
HANS CHRISTIAN ANDERSEN

'A fresh new translation of these two classic fairy tales recreates the
lyrical beauty and pathos of the Danish genius' evergreen stories'
The Bay

THE CAT WHO CAME IN OFF THE ROOF
ANNIE M.G. SCHMIDT

'Guaranteed to make anyone 7-plus to 107 who likes to
curl up with a book and a cat purr with pleasure'
The Times

LAFCADIO: THE LION WHO SHOT BACK
SHEL SILVERSTEIN

'A story which is really funny, yet also teaches us a great
deal about what we want, what we think we want and what
we are no longer certain about once we have it'
Irish Times

THE SECRET OF THE BLUE GLASS
TOMIKO INUI

'I love this book... How important it is, in these times, that our children
read the stories from other peoples, other cultures, other times'
Michael Morpurgo, *Guardian*

THE STORY OF THE BLUE PLANET
ANDRI SNÆR MAGNASON

Illustrated by Áslaug Jónsdóttir

'A Seussian mix of wonder, wit and gravitas'
The New York Times